YOUR SALT ON MY LIPS

YOUR SALT ON MY LIPS

(mostly) queer literary erotica

BY

Liz Asch

This is a 2nd edition with two added stories.

ARS SALUTARIA PRESS
Copyright © 2022 by Ars Salutaria Press
Copyright © 2023 renewed by Liz Asch

"An Interplay of Oppositions" originally ran as "After Class" in *BUST Magazine's* One-Handed Read column (July 2016). "Entre Nous" was published in *Begging for It: Erotic Fantasies for Women* (Rachel Kramer Bussel, ed, Cleis Press, 2016).

Funding for the original print version of this book came from Oregon's Regional Arts & Culture Council. Much appreciation and gratitude to RACC.

ISBN 979-8-218-13740-3

Cover art by Liz Asch
Design and layout by Alissa Beddow
Printed in the USA

Published February 2023

Author's Note

THIS BOOK IS written for your body. For your hands, for your eyes, for your skin, for your sex. It is written for your senses, your tongue, your fingertips, and your sexual expression. May these stories ignite your libido and your imagination, support your empowerment, and stoke your desires.

Table of Contents

Mouthing an Orchid

WHEN I FINALLY see you after all this time, I'll let you make the first move. I'll be in shock, in awe, I'll feel numb and dumb, I know it. I'll come to you, and there will be this awkward pause when I don't know whether to kiss you, cup your face and stare at you, or wrap my arms around you. We'll hug. We'll hold each other a long time and I'll let you kiss me first. That's what we've agreed to.

How will we first fuck again? Slow and languorous, saturated with love? Or fast and furious, driven by wild lust? Presumably, some of each. Will we make out first, or go straight for the cunt?

I can see it in my mind's eye. It's a movie I turn on and play obsessively, one that fills my body with tingles and makes my heart let loose like a balloon. I get breathless watching it, turned on and wet. My hands hold your jaw and turn your face so that I can admire every angle of your gorgeous face and kiss you—along your cheekbones, your eyelids, your temples, your nose, the corners of your mouth, your chin. And your lips. I'll bring your sweet tongue into my mouth and pull and suck and lick and swallow you. This is one language we share, this hot and humid, sweet and spicy dance of endless kissing.

But for now . . . I see my hands moving down your neck, fingers trailing, your mouth gaping open, my mouth coming to bite your neck, nibble your ears. You've always loved that. I see you writhe your hips and arch your back. I slip my finger down to your cunt to feel how slick you've gotten already. You whimper. I move my finger to trail down one inner thigh while I keep licking your neck, your collarbone, your sternum, and now one nipple.

Do you know how long I've waited to have these nipples in my mouth again? Gorgeous brown nipples, small-tipped, areolas like the sun. Dewey, dipped, luscious tits. I've been dreaming of them. I've been jacking off to them for months. I've been waiting for those nipples to rest lightly between my teeth, for my tongue to run circles and my lips to suck. I've been waiting for you. I've been so patient. Panting, and heaving, and moaning, and imagining all this time.

My fingers will run down your ribcage, scratching lightly, not too hard, unless you like that, I'll have to see. I'll be watching you like a hawk to see what you like, what revs you up the most, and I'll be listening to every sound you make for clues. I want to learn it all so that I can send you over the edge whenever I want. So that I can drive you like a little gadget I command into the throes of passion. You hear that, baby? I'll be taking copious notes. Some of what we'll learn you don't even know about yourself yet. We will learn together. About you and me.

For now, though, I've moved my hands down to stroke your phenomenal thighs. I fucking love thick thighs, and yours are the most magnificent I've ever seen. I run my hands around and grab ahold of them, pushing myself away from the magnetic draw of your pussy. You get a great view of my tits like this, and I watch you watch me arch my back while I squeeze your thighs. From here I can watch your pussy sweat, knowing what's coming. I brush lightly against you and breathe on you and inhale your ripening scent and then pull away, making you wait a little longer. I stall by massaging your thighs, gripping my hands only partway around their girth.

But I can't resist, so I lower myself down to kiss your pussy just as I would your mouth. A soft, sensual, slow, deep taste kind of first kiss. You shudder. And I press your thighs harder. I run my tits over your cunt and your belly, up your chest, and against your lips. And then I return to the prize. This, the flower between your legs. To love you is to mouth an orchid. I will envelop your petals. I will lick you inside and out. I will discover with my tongue every stroke and circle and pressure point and rhythm that drives you wild. My mouth will kiss your pussy the way one sucks a passionfruit for pulp, sweet seeds, and sticky juice.

You will become undone in my hands.

We're just getting started.

My fingers toy with your fat pussy lips while I climb onto your thigh and rub against it with my salivating cunt. You love that. I know because you give me that look before you close your eyes and tip your head back in the kind of extreme pleasure that requires such a breach of eye contact. I take that as my opportunity to run my finger down the slick swollen ruffles of your pussy and dip into the little hole that awaits our union.

I'm riding your thigh while I start to fuck you with my finger, just one for a while, in and out, and deeper and deeper, and I wait for you to ask me to add another finger. I want you to be able to tell me what you want, baby. You reach for my cunt. That's what you want. You want us both to finger each other while I ride your thigh. You've been waiting so patiently for this arrangement of our bodies in love, and I want to give you everything you want. You lick your finger and give me the look that you are coming to fuck me, and I start to breathe really heavily. I focus on how amazing it feels to be inside you so that I don't faint. Your wet finger slips inside me, and I nearly collapse. Steady, steady. I moan, loudly, and rub myself harder against you, covering your thigh in a shiny runway of my juices.

We are each deep inside the other. I ask for more fingers, and then more. And you are riding my hand so hard. And we are sweaty, eyes bulging, tits swinging, mouths agape. I love you, I love you, I love you we croon.

Our climaxes start to build at the same time. My moaning gets more animalistic, and my body starts to lose its rhythm. Yours doesn't. You keep fucking me firmly—you're pouring all of your love from your heart into your hand into my cunt, and I can feel it exploding like a supernova inside me. I'm losing my shit. I start to wail.

You start to pant, quick and breathy, and our fingers just keep fucking each other, and you are moaning now, and I am screaming now, my pussy clenching your fingers in spasms. And I'm cumming on your thigh, the sheets, your belly, your arm. It's gushing with each thrust, and you start to chant *ohmygod ohmygod ohmyfucking god*. You keep fucking me because you are exactly the lover I want and have always wanted. The tenacious one. The one with everlasting biceps. The one who would move a boulder if it was in my way. You keep fucking me, through the spasms, through the tidal waves.

My fingers are hooked inside you and I'm not going anywhere. I can feel how hot and swollen you are. I've got my thumb rubbing against your clit while I fuck you, and it's building inside you, I can feel it. Your mouth gets that one shape it only gets when you cum, and you writhe up against my hand, pumping and rubbing, and flailing and clenching—until you grab my hand and hold it, telling me to stop, *stop,* while your body flops back against the bed. My hand stays inside you. Your eyes are dreamy and wet, and our bodies are covered in cum. Your hand is still inside me. "More, baby?" you ask, love in your voice, in your eyes, in your heart.

Hello, Sailor

WHENEVER WE COULD, we'd meet in the forest, back where the old wartime bunkers were hidden in the trees. Old scrappy metal holes in the sides of the hills, rusty doors and little caverns, just the right amount of privacy in the outdoors for me to pound my cock into your little cavern with my hand over your mouth so that you'd stay quiet.

Ours was a dark romance, witnessed only by the owls and the rustling nests of deer dreaming in the brush. We were held captive by the laws of the military, unable to be together on the base or in public for fear of being seen. But, hot damn, did my prick stiffen in my uniform every time you walked by.

Your ass snug in your Service Dress, penis pressed behind the zipper I longed to unlock with my teeth. Those broad shoulders and the little curls of hair that tufted out of your shorts and ran down your legs. The smell of you, cumin, and motor oil oozing in the sun.

"Down on your knees," I'd ordered the first time.

"No, sir, no," you'd pretend pleaded.

A shit-eating grin on your face.

Sometimes when I would fuck you, I'd whisper in your ear. I'd say the most tender things I could think of, loving and soft and sweet, because we never got enough of that. I called you baby and told you I wished I could take you away from all this, feed you strawberries in a bed of white linen with the soft sun kissing the windows and the sea whistling in the wind just waiting for us to swim, for me to towel you dry and bring you inside, light a fire, and kiss every square inch of your body in the dark orange light.

Sometimes when you were fucking me, you'd whisper stories in my ear, scenes of our lovemaking throughout history, imagining we were servants meeting up in secret in the stables, and Shakespearean lovers who had a dungeon squirreled away underground where we did debaucherous things to each other.

Once you pretended we were two maidens at a fancy dance, who had both been asked to waltz by the most eligible bachelors in the room. They whisked us around in our ballgowns, and we kept making eye contact over their shoulders, sending each other indications of desire. The heat between us was building. You excused yourself first and then I followed. We met in a broom closet, where you unlaced my bodice and slipped your fingers inside, rubbing my nipples and kissing my neck. You spoke of the way you climbed under my gown and slipped off my bloomers, as you took me into your mouth and, laying your lips there, brought me a new, bright pleasure. We grew ravenous, hidden in our small, dirty forest lair, reinventing our bodies in that broom closet. Your words brought me rapture, as I switched electrically between male and female, feeling it all, in the cold night air and in the conjured warmth of the broom closet. You got me so turned on that when you grabbed my chest and twisted my nipples, I came into your hand while your cock was throbbing inside my ass.

I want to be your servant. I want to be your king. I want you inside me as deep as I can take it. I want your fingers, your whole hand, your tongue, your lips, your sex. If you let me, I can be your anything and everything.

Dream with me, lover. Write another story, please. Hold me here, now, against your chest, and make the world slow to a stop.

In the Lemon Tree

ALL I CAN think about is yellow. Lemons. Light.

I am five, in California, alone with a backyard lemon tree. It is a kingdom, this tree, and its essence is sinking into my skin.

First the lemons wag at me from high in the branches. They peek out from the leaves like shiny treasures. Unreachable. Glowing yellow trophies dancing high on display, their plump bodies riding the breeze. Lemons winking at me from the treetops. Raining a mist of sweet fragrance. Light dances through the leaves, making lacy patterns on my knees. My hand reaches to touch the bark of the trunk. It is warm like skin.

The air cools and warms again, the ground freezes and thaws, again and again and again. I'm ten years old.

Light edges my body. The gleaming lines of my arms reaching, my neck tipped back, openmouthed to the sky. Rays of sun flickering into my eyes. Lemons bobbing radiantly in the leaves and the light. In my heart there's a glinting flame, growing.

A cool relief of a cloud passing over the tree and then the sun shining hotter, brighter. Light flushes through my body and illuminates my knees, leaps to my face in a rush. I bend back further, extending my gaze, and my chest stretches as if it could crack, dislodge a bird from a cage, a bird that could fly up into this tree above me, around me. This tree that is in me. This tree is me. I'm turning transparent. I'm falling in. My body against the tree, limp, melted, and every cell buzzing high. My vision goes. Black to yellow sunspots. The dappled light dancing warm and cool on my skin, the breeze kissing my inner elbows, the backs of my knees. The air is just a thing to hold me together.

Twelve.

I'm slipping into something invisible. I'm losing the lines that define me. The land of lemons. It is not of this place. It is not here. I am in the arms of the lemon tree, melting into its sweet peppery hold. My tongue arches to the roof of my mouth, my teeth sparkle with sharp hunger. The lemons cling to their branches with a tighter grip. They feel my pull and they're fighting. They know they are squeezable and filled with a precious elixir that I crave. They sway and tighten their pucker to the stem that feeds them.

No one knows I'm here.

I am older now, fifteen. The tree stands as it did before. My fingertips reach to brush the lowest branches.

If I could just have them—their cool dimpled skin in my palms, their little bodies against my lips. I want to scratch into their skins and watch the oil bead. I want to twist them, gnash them open, and sip their juicy spill, feel their pebbled flesh gleaming in the pocket of my cheek. I want to suck each seed, rolling it up the roof of my mouth with my tongue, sliding the pebble of it down my throat, sensing its slinking exploration to a part of me I cannot reach. Come into me. Fall. Slip down my tunnel. Slide into my stomach and boil inside of me.

At twenty now, my body knows itself anew, knows its place in the tree. My hands unfurl from the branches of my arms, from their root in my heart. My fingers are reaching to grab, pluck, twist, envelop, and eradicate each lemon. To nip each fruit from its stem and entangle it into my existence. I can break its suckered hold and take it. It will breathe in my breath as I taste it. I want it held deep within me. A seed inside me. A seed inside it. Seed upon seed upon seed. And when each seed blooms—a glorious unfolding. A concert of waves roiling. A loosening in my body that shakes me, dropping my seeds, my leaves, my lemons, the layers unfolding like a canopy of leaves.

I'm suspended between the sky and the earth. My breath is a yellow dripping scent. My skin is a halo of light. Lemon is an oil I carry rich in my skin, snaked through the hold of each muscle. Droplets of yellow lace through my body, a web under my skin.

The air is waiting. Glasses clink from inside the house. Chatter and the sound of moving bodies stepping into the yard. I'm here in the tree, entangled in branches. The spotted shadows blinking. The scorch of sunlight singeing the tender surface off the leaves.

Girls on Top

DILDO RODEO
LAST SATURDAY OF MONTH
11 PM
GIRLS ON TOP

We saw the flyer posted on a telephone pole on Christopher Street, and, oh, we were going. Girls on Top was the best dyke bar in the West Village, and we all wanted to go to the infamous Dildo Rodeo night. According to legend, you were likely to get in if you were super cute or very sexy or extremely nice. You could flirt like mad with the big butch bouncer, hoping she'd unlock the velvet rope for you. Dixie and I met all three criteria, so I figured it should be no problem, but still I felt a small flutter in my chest. What if we got turned away? We strategized. Just in case we had any trouble, Dixie had brought along a little bribery grab bag of sex toys from her shop. She was always getting freebies from companies hoping she'd sell their products in her store, so she had plenty to give. She'd give the bouncer anything.

We waited in line for an hour, delighting in the people watching, trying to be discreet when we noticed someone hot, or especially silly, or maybe famous. I tried to make eyes at the bouncer a few times, but she had the focus of a racehorse. She wore those funny 80s glasses with black plastic slats on them, so that she could see your eyes but you couldn't see hers. She might as well have been wearing blinders. I started to imagine her tacked up like a horse, strapped in a bridle and reins, a metal bit in her mouth, wearing those blinders. Hot. Oh, I could ride her.

We got to the front of the line and I just looked at her as if she were saddled and ready to go. As if in the mirror of my eye she might see me riding her. Me, in my smart, tight riding gear, chaps, and a black velvet helmet, straddling her, her wild, long neck chained to my reins. We paused like that, and I let the image run between us like a zoetrope in my pupils. Could she see it? Could she feel it? Next to me, Dixie flirted and chirped and pushed a handful of toys into her hand—lube bottles, clit stims, and pocket vibrators. The bouncer waved us through, her nose still pointed in my direction. I could imagine her sizing me up and down. I leaned in as I passed her by to smell the strength coming off her. I cast a secret wish to see her later.

Inside it was dark and crowded. The walls were cluttered with memorabilia—black-and-white photos of old timey cowgirls in hiked-up blue jeans, Rosie the Riveter with her big fist and stern sparkling eyes, do-wop girls on the stage, Wonder Woman swinging a lasso high above her big hair, vintage college girls with their arms around each other's tiny waists, nudes with big tits and big hips, flappers with spit curls on their foreheads, and ads from the fifties about vibrators and exercise machines. The place was crowded with people—all kinds of people, all genders, some all femmed up in glitter and big hair, some in masculine dress, some half-dressed, some barely dressed. There were little scruffy punk kids, foxy lipstick lesbians, tough girls, badass old butches, studs in leather vests, young queer gender benders, twinks in cut-off Ts and short shorts, iconic ballroom queens—some of everyone was there.

A spotlight gleamed down to the center of the room, where you could just catch a glimpse of the bull, a tuft of auburn hair and a wild glass eye. The room smelled of heavy sweat and leather oil. You could taste it on your tongue, its fumes running circles in your mouth.

Dixie and I careened through the crowd, making our way to the bull. We wanted to see it up close. It was on a raised center stage the size of a small boxing ring. Ropes blocked off the square of it, wrapped around posts at each corner. The saddle was dark brown, a shiny hard leather, newly oiled and almost steaming under the heat of the spotlight. The animal was made of real pelt—warmed by the spotlight as if by the sun, with a curly tangle of hair on its wide head. Two shapely horns stretched out from either side like a pair of splayed legs. It was as heavy and solid as a truck. Its hooves perched like sharp little dancer feet a few inches above the floor. Drop a few quarters in, and it would go. But, for now, it rested there, impossibly still. Its wildness hidden away, as tame as a stone.

The emcee was a famous drag king who went by the name of Slim Swooney, and just about every girl I knew madly wanted to be swept away by her wily charms and strong arms. She was a mysterious boy-ish girl who was all muscle and charisma and dazzle, with a delicate chiseled face and a head of curly black locks spilled into a fauxhawk with shaved sides. Bright, hard, white teeth. Coy curling lips. Bronze skin. Thick lashes. A white tank top slung itself over Slim's shoulders, kissed her tiny gorgeous tits and hugged her waist. Her black leather pants hung low at her hips and tight around her ass. Slim was a fucking magnet for eyes of all genders and sexualities. She just oozed sensuality, effortlessly, as if she was made of it up to her ears. Her eyes were a rich, deep brown, touched with a glint of mischief, always.

The moment Slim Swooney came up to the platform with a rhine-stone-studded mic in her hand and a sultry swing in her hips, the crowd hushed. All eyes were on the line of Slim's pants barely hanging on to their low ride on the crest of her hips, like we were waiting for some precious cargo ship to come up over the undulating line of that black leather horizon and save us with its abundant provisions. Slim leaned over to inspect the bull. She put her strong, thin hand on its back and peered underneath. The black leather slickness of her pants grabbed her ass. Gasps escaped from the crowd as several spectators allowed them-selves to contemplate Slim's cunt, wedged among those black leather ripples, and the valley of her ass crack.

Slim turned to tug a rope here and there. She paced the stage in her shiny cowboy boots. We watched her motion with her well-tuned fingers to someone in the crowd. An assistant scrambled up, a little girly gurrl with ratty white-blonde ponytails and teeny scout shorts, a blue bikini top speckled with stars, and black suspenders. She stepped forward in her tall socks and bowling shoes and buckled a black leather harness onto the saddle. The metal ring gleamed under the shine of the spotlight like a circle of diamonds.

The crowd was getting thick. Dixie and I were caught in the front, wedged up against a couple of bear guys with thick, furry necks and a gaggle of shirtless boys in hot pants. A sophisticated lesbian couple stood to our left, the grey-haired one fussing with a fancy camera. I squeezed Dixie's hand as the lights went dim and a disco ball started to spin, swirling sparkles around the room.

Slim Swooney crooned to us the night's agenda, her voice intimate and deliberate, as if any one of us were her lover receiving her instructions in the sanctity of her dark bedroom. "Everyone gets ten minutes. If you don't need that much, we'll let you off early. Rapunzel feeds quarters into the machine for you. Performers, you will each bring your own dildo, your own lube if you need it, all your own supplies. We clean up while you rest up. Then, on to the next performer. Best of show (by applause) wins a goody bag."

Slim held up a burlap sack, marked with a big black question mark. "Giddy-up!" Slim hollered, and she smacked the bull on the ass. A giant jug of quarters rested by the corner of the stage, where the machine part was. Rapunzel, the girl in suspenders, stood at the ready, her fingers locked on the first quarter.

First up was Shae Gamoré. She was tan and blonde with big tits bulging out from under a tiny brown leather vest, jean cut-offs frayed at the tops of her thighs. Tall cowgirl boots with white stars spray-painted all over them. The lights dazzled and a blast of music shot into the air, filling the room as if to surround Shae, who was running her fingers through her long blonde hair and tipping her head back. She smiled wryly at the crowd and tapped the heel of her cowgirl boot in time to the music. Shae's legs were long and lean and tan. She pulled a hot pink glassy dildo from her white leather handbag and buckled it into the harness. She patted the bull, circled the stage, kicked off her cowgirl boots, and unbuttoned her pants. Her little jean shorts slipped to the floor.

Shae was sporting a shaved snatch with a tattoo over her pubic bone that read *Mine* in cursive. The music boomed above us, around Shae. She climbed atop the bull and balanced her slim feet along the bull's spine, like a surfer girl looking for her next wave. The dildo bobbed in the air, awaiting Shae.

There was a rope hanging from the ceiling that I hadn't noticed before, and Shae grabbed ahold of it for balance. She was dancing now like the best kind of stripper, swinging her hips and wagging her ass. All of us were held captive by her every movement, noting the distance that was slowly shrinking between the dildo and Shae's slit. Once Shae had us all turned on, she turned herself on. Squatting atop the bull's back, she teased herself with the head of the dildo, moving up and down an inch or so, while her arm reached up to hang onto the rope for balance. And then she let go. Shae surrendered and sunk her body onto the dildo with a huge moan. She leaned over the bull's back, mashed her tits into its neck, grabbed hold of the horns, and motioned to Rapunzel, *Go.*

Everyone was imagining that long dildo wedged way up inside of Shae and the relentless fuck she was about to take. Rapunzel plunked the quarters in, and the machine started to buzz and rollick. As the bull undulated, Shae's ass started to quiver. Shae opened her mouth and wailed and squinched her face, hanging onto the bull as it bucked beneath her, slamming her with the cock and buzzing her thighs to a pulp. She hooked her feet into the stirrups and hoisted her ass in the air, so that we could see the pink dildo slipping in and out of her slit so fast and hard, and we could hear the slap of her ass against the saddle. Fucking Shae!

Her knuckles were white, gripping the horns. She was gasping and moaning and panting, and her long legs were shaking in the stirrups. She gritted her teeth as her tits bounced so furiously they spilled up and over that tight little leather vest. Her nipples were grazing the bull's fur with every thrust. She didn't last long. Shae came hard and sloshy, like a waterfall poured over the bull's back, with yips and gasps and one loud scream.

Rapunzel, well-trained, saw it coming and pushed the stop button, so the machine would slow to a creak while Shae recovered, limp, slung on the bull's back, her fingers gripping the saddle. The crowd roared. Shae sat up, blinking, smiling, tried to artfully stand up and remove herself from the dildo. But you could tell she was a pile of mush. When she dismounted and bowed her curtsy, her hair was a wreck and her make-up all smeared. Her nipples still flounced over the vest. Shae removed her pink dildo with dignity, kissed it a victory kiss, and stepped off the stage with wobbly legs.

A team of stagehands swept in and cleaned off the bull, while the rest of us yearned for a hand job. My head felt strangely empty. Was I in shock? But it was a pleasant feeling, so nice to think of nothing, but to have only this feeling, this kind of dazed splendor inside. Between my legs a wet buzz lingered, a warm spread. I wondered if I could cum just from watching this thing.

Next.

Slim's voice glided through the darkness to introduce, "Jaaaaah-pah-loh! The most dangerous boi-boy from the West Indies that you would ever dare to meet because he could kill you with his good looks and the clench of his murderous ass. Get ready!"

When Japallo stepped onto the stage, it was as if Cleopatra herself had appeared on a gurney carried by a herd of half-man, half-antelopes and trailed by a flock of golden swans. Japallo took our breath away. Six feet tall, dark black, all muscle, and cinched into a glimmering gold spandex unitard. His gleaming suit came down to his calves and wrists, and wrapped up and over his sculpted shoulders to stretch over his head like an alien. There was a large circle for his face, and a matching cut-out over his ass.

Japallo's music came on the loudspeakers, and he started to vibrate and shake his ass on hyperspeed as he circled the bull. He pressed his wide palms against the bull's back and stuck his quivering, thrusting ass way far out, and then turned and arched his back to rub it, staccato, all over the bull's flanks. Thankfully, the stage began to spin like a slow lazy Susan so that everyone could see. This was not something anyone should ever miss.

Then, Japallo touched the sharp tip of the bull's horn to his long tongue and licked the length of the horn. He danced over to a gold leather bag at the corner of the stage and pulled out a gleaming golden cock. He licked it too and then rubbed it between his thighs and down the crack of his ass. He inched it around the cut-out circle around his ass. We could see the tip of it nosing around the circle under the tight spandex, and something about it was so suggestive it got me extra hot. Then he licked the base of the cock and stuffed the whole thing into his mouth. He ran his tongue around it—you could see it through his cheek—and when he pulled it out, it was glistening with saliva. Japallo strapped the cock onto the harness of the saddle and spit on it hard. It stood there dripping, in that all too familiar way.

He motioned to Rapunzel to turn it on, and the bull started to roil.

As the bull rocked, and the cock vibrated, Japallo stood tall and gleaming, looking like a fucking Oscar statue, one long slender foot on the bull's neck and one balanced high on its rump. He motioned to the audience, and a tiny gold bottle flew through the air into his large open palm. He tipped the bottle upside down and squirted a long shot of lube onto the shaking cock. He then leaned over, agile as a yogi, his ass beaming, and began to give the cock a hand job, distributing the lube and giving everyone in the room an even bigger surge.

He tossed the bottle back into the dark room towards wherever it came from, where a rustle of bodies fought for immediate ownership. On stage, Japallo's gorgeous muscled ass was hovering in the air, quivering. He was making us wait. Just a little. And then he did the unthinkable.

On top of a bucking bull, with a dildo tremoring like a conductor's baton instructing vibrato, Japallo leapt onto the bull's back, arched his body into a backbend, and slid that golden cock right into the bull-seye of his ass. He tipped his head back, making it look like a large golden egg nestled in its auburn nest. On his face, the upside down contortion of extreme exertion and pleasure. His hips scooted back and forth magnificently against the waves of the bull's spasmodic rocking.

You could see the tiny peaks of his nipples under the tight stretch of spandex. You could see his eyes unfocused and lolling into some other place. The thin line of his gums were exposed from under his upper lip, snagged loosely in a snarl of ecstasy.

Everything felt topsy-turvy. Japallo bent over the bull, a strap-on on a saddle on a bull fucking a golden ass, Rapunzel maniacally feeding the machine quarters—and then, it all came to a slow halt. A *bleep bleep bleep* went off with a swirl of disco lights, and the bull heaved to a halt. Japallo rested for a moment, his arch sinking, and then he came back to us like a dancer, lowering his long legs and whipping his spine gracefully vertical. Still sitting on the cock, he spun around for us, evoking another gasp from the audience, paused in a classic riding pose, and grasped the bull by the horns and kissed the top of its curly head. He then unsnapped the harness and hopped off, with the dildo still clutched in his ass! He waved a large palm at us as he circled the stage and made small bows, the crowd hooting and hollering until long after he was gone.

Dixie and I turned to face each other with wide eyes, our mouths mirroring the other's astonishment. It was so all intense! We gripped each other's hands and tumbled into each other, struggling to regain composure. What kind of experience was this!? We had thought we were prepared, but we had no idea.

Once again, a team of stagehand hygienists dressed in all black were all over the bull like a pack of flies, with bobbing headlamps, getting it ready for the next performance. The crowd was abuzz with noise, laughter, and chatter.

As the lights dimmed and the crowd quieted, Dixie and I glanced at each other and squeezed hands, wondering what could possibly come next. I considered the state of my sopping underwear and wondered if I could withstand another round without a splotch showing through.

Up next was a threesome who called themselves the Backseat Boys. When Slim introduced them, three small, well-built young men in tight, solid-colored briefs came running up to the stage. They began to cartwheel, their brown, tan, and olive legs spinning Vs in tandem. Then they chased each other around the bull, playing hot potato with a giant, thick-veined dildo, the kind that looks *very* realistic. The boy band song "Everybody" blasted through the speakers, sounding at first like an electronic dance song, and then shifting into that familiar pop slop.

The gymnasts started taunting each other with the dildo, making it hard to get, all trying to grab it from the others' hands. One of them sneaked the dildo into the harness and then the other two jumped on him, tussling and wrestling on the floor of the stage between and around the prancing hooves of the bull. Then the tussling turned to tumbling and bouncing, and then into an acrobatic dance routine.

Individuated by the color of their briefs, Red, Yellow, and Aqua bopped around each other, taking turns to bolt up onto the back of the bull, lick the dildo, or grind suggestively against it, before springing back down to the stage, all tightly choreographed to the music. Their compact asses and packages flashed as they worked their gymnastic moves. They were all mesmerizing and crazy hot.

Yellow did a dance solo perched on top of the bull. He was a foxy go-go boy with short dreads, pierced nipples on his narrow, brown chest, and a sweet grin that oozed confidence. He gave the giant dildo a long, drawn-out hand job, slow and then lightning fast. I felt my crotch get crazy hot, then suddenly numb. He kept time to the music, pumping his tiny butt in the air and jerking his slim hips back and forth.

"Geez," Dixie whistled through her teeth. I wondered if Dixie knew before today that gay male sex turned her on. I had to assume this was news to her. It was not news to me. This performance was as impressive and effective on me as I would have guessed it would be upon hearing a description.

When Yellow dismounted, Red hopped up, straddling the bull's rump like a gymnast on a vault. He swung his legs back and forth, rubbing his crotch against the ridge of the bull's spine. His back, chest, and arms were hairy and tanned and scripted with tattoos, which rippled as he grasped the back edge of the saddle. He was really humping it, his legs all muscled and strong. Again, I heard Dixie grunt something incoherent. But I couldn't, or wouldn't, take my eyes off the stage to check on her.

When Red was sufficiently turned on, you could see his shorts bulging like an animal was trapped in there. He backwards somersaulted off the bull in a perfect dismount, turned around, and started making out with Yellow against the side of the bull. Their lithe hips ground against that auburn animal pelt. Yellow's hands gripping the waistband of Red's shorts. Red's mouth on Yellow's nipple ring. And then it got even better. The song shifted to a boy band remix, some snappy, clubby beat, and Aqua mounted the bull. Red and Yellow disappeared into the shadows to give Aqua the limelight.

Aqua struck a gymnast's pose, arms lifted, toes pointed, stretched out. He tipped himself effortlessly into a handstand, balanced and centered over the saddle, his shiny black hair grazing the bull's neck fur. He arched his smooth chest, tipped his head to the side, opened his pretty lips, and began to blow the dildo, licking it slowly at first and then cramming it into his mouth. An upside down blow! I couldn't believe it. He was giving this huge cock seriously good bottom-up head, his arms shaking with strength and fatigue, his toes still pointed high up in the air, his ass clenched in balance mode.

His whole body was quivering when Red climbed aboard and grabbed upside-down Aqua by the hips. He flipped him deftly over his head and onto his shoulders, like a little kid, or a cheerleader, and then Yellow sprung up onto the bull, grabbed the rope, and climbed up onto

Aqua's shoulders. A threesome stack of hot boys in tight undies on a bull! Aqua, in the middle, inched a one-eighty so that his crotch went into the face of Red, and Yellow's crotch went into his face. Then the whole tower of them started grinding and thrusting to the music, while they nuzzled each other's crotches. What a finale!

Somehow they had snatched the dildo off the saddle as they built their pyramid, and Red, on the bottom, with one hand grasping Aqua tight to his face, had the other hand around the dildo and was pumping it in the air to the music. The lights went out and the applause grew as the tower of three unbelievably talented hotties dismounted and trotted through the crowd back to the dressing room, to do, I suppose, any number of things, which I could only shudder to imagine.

It was intermission. Which was good, because everyone needed a cigarette break. Dixie and I stumbled out from the dark, steamy club and poured, with the rest of the crowd, into the street. "Let's take a little walk," I suggested, and we numbly tottered around the corner. We figured we had time to catch a breath of fresh air and gather ourselves together a bit before Act Two began. It was late night in the West Village and the city was a flurry of commotion: people laughing in clusters tumbling down the street, tchotchkes hawked on the sidewalks, short shorts gripping the hard plastic perfect asses of models in storefronts, pizza dough tossed like flabby parachutes into oregano air.

Dixie and I hardly talked. What was there to say? We'd both seen it all. As my wobbly legs carried me through the bustling sidewalk lit with glimmering lights, my mind started wandering back to the club. What was Slim Swooney doing now? Who got to spend intermission with her? And what about that trio of boys, what were they up to in their dressing room?

Would I ever have the courage to get up on a stage like that?

Or get with someone who had?

She Touches Herself

SHE STARTS BY rubbing her tits and belly. She runs her hands over her hips and between her thighs. She circles the vibrator over her nipples. Her hand reaches down to her cunt and she runs her middle finger up and down the crest of lips. She pauses her fingertip at the crux, where the lips split like theater curtains, and she starts to rub in a circular motion. Her mouth opens. She closes her eyes. Her other hand moves the vibrator around her nipples. She rubs furiously with one finger, then another, changing the tempo and the direction, and then she pauses, catching her breath. She brings that hand to her mouth, inhales the scent, and licks her fingers. The fingers go into her cunt, in and out, in and out. Her legs are spread wide. She brings the vibrator down to her mons and presses it there. She rubs it back and forth over her clit while fucking herself with her fingers. *Ohhhh*, she moans. Her forehead is sweating. Her tits jiggle. The lips of her pussy expose little pink petals as she gyrates her hand in and out. Her inner thighs shine with fluid. She keeps moving her hand and shaking the vibrator, pressing it harder and harder against her pubic bone. She gasps when she cums and grits her teeth. Her thighs quake through the climax. You can see her pussy panting around her fingers. She calms and removes her hand, bringing it to her face to smell the glorious scent and then letting her hand flop onto her belly. She rests a minute, her eyes closed, a sleepy smile on her lips. Then, she opens her eyes and lifts the vibrator back to her clit. She begins again. And then, after that, again.

At Home After Hours

WHEN MAX KNOCKED softly at the door, I tiptoed down the steps and turned the knob slowly to avoid a loud creak. He was wearing some kind of herbal cologne and held a droopy yard flower in his hand.

"Thanks," I said. "I'll put this in water. It's nice to see you."

Max smiled and stood there on the stoop.

"I'm glad you wanted to come over," I added.

"Glad to be here," he said, still standing in the doorway. "Asleep?" he asked, referring to my toddler, whom I had just put to bed.

"Asleep!" I confirmed, and I took his hand and drew him inside. "What would you like to drink?" I asked. "Tea, seltzer, fruit spritzer?" Max was sober and I liked to give him a few options other than water.

"Mmm, herbal tea," he purred, sticking close to me in the kitchen.

"Honey?" I asked.

"Yes, honey," he answered. "Always."

I asked Max to put on a record, and he chose Etta James and put it on low, and we placed our cups of tea on the coffee-table and settled into the sofa.

After a little small talk I asked, "So how did that feel last time?"

I was referring to earlier that month when I'd hosted a small dinner party and Max had stayed late to help me clean up, and then as he was leaving, we'd kissed in the doorway for a while and then talked briefly about wanting to do that again. We'd texted a little bit and come up with this plan of him coming over after Ethan went to bed. It was only eight o'clock. The night was young.

"It felt really nice," Max said, looking right into my eyes and reaching for my hand. He started to stroke my wrist and fingers lightly with his. My insides flung up and fluttered down. Max was so fucking cute.

"You're really sweet," I said, feeling excited and shy, and telling myself to take it slowly. The last person I hooked up with, I literally leapt into her lap and straddled her on this same couch within moments of our first kiss. *Too much, too fast,* I cautioned myself. *Feel it out with him.*

I had to slow down for me, and also for Max. While we were doing the dishes and wiping down the table that night after the party, Max shared with me that he hadn't been with anyone yet since his top surgery a few months ago. He explained that now that his scars were healed, he knew it would feel different to be close with someone. I hoped that he wanted to get closer to me.

"Do you feel comfortable kissing me again?" I asked.

"Yes," Max said. "But first I'd like to keep doing this, is that all right?" he asked as he ran his fingers lightly up my arms. "And this?" he asked, as he ran his hands over my collarbone.

I nodded, looking right into his eyes, sighing. It felt so good.

"May I touch you, too?" I asked.

"Yes," he said softly. "Please."

I placed my fingertips on Max's shoulders and ran one hand down each arm and over his palm, making my fingers soft and light, and really feeling his energy. He moaned happily.

"Legs?" I asked. He smiled and nodded.

I started mid-thigh, careful to stay low and slow, and again ran soft hands over his legs, all the way to the instep of his feet. I did that a few more times, changing up the speed and pressure a little each time. Max looked like a puppy basking in the sun.

"Hug?" I asked.

"Yes," he agreed sleepily.

I came up close and brushed my cheek against his, came close to his neck but didn't kiss it. I just breathed him in a little, and we pressed our chests together. It felt so damn good. His body was warm with a steady pulse of energy that felt like it was thumping alongside mine.

Our chests stayed connected and we nuzzled each other, still without kissing.

He breathed in my ear, "Would you like your shirt off?"

"Yes," I whispered back. "Would you like yours off?"

"Yes."

Max started undoing the buttons on my blouse and slipped it off. He traced down my cleavage with his finger. He hugged my waist and tipped his pelvis toward mine, and I moaned. I ran my hands around his waist, finding a trail of hair seductively snaking down from his navel. I moved my hands up the sides of his ribcage and looked into his eyes before lifting his t-shirt. *Yes*, his eyes indicated, *go ahead.* I slid his shirt over his head, and Max smiled with pride. It struck me that he was liberated, free to go around shirtless. Then my eyes met Max's chest scars. My heart slipped, melted into a puddle, and sizzled like firecrackers. I felt awash with a lust I hadn't anticipated. Here was the body he belonged in, and he took these major steps to make it so. Something about that activated in me a primal sense of passion. I wanted to take Max every which way and slather his chest with my tongue, my breasts, my pussy lips. I wanted to devour him. I had to hold back.

Deep breath. *Don't ravage without consent,* I told myself.

Look in his eyes.

"May I kiss your chest?" I asked.

Max nodded and stroked my cheek. It was such a surprisingly tender gesture. Then, he unclasped my bra and it hung trapped between us while I lowered my mouth to his scars. First, I just brushed my lips, barely touching his skin, tracing the curve of one scar and then the other, letting him feel the closeness of me with hardly any contact, mostly my breath.

"How's that feel?" I murmured close.

"Good," Max breathed. He was watching me lick his scars. He jutted his chest out and flexed his muscles. So hot. I played with the pressure, letting my lips touch a little more as he got used to it. Then I ran a wide circle of my tongue around his nipples and I came a little in my pants. It just happened. I completely could not control it. My pussy spasmed and it just rolled through me. I stopped in my tracks as my body clenched. I looked up at Max. He was getting off watching me, and he whispered, "Keep going."

I wanted to suck him, to bite him, but I didn't want to overwhelm. I inhaled his hairy armpit and let the sexy sweat aroma waft into my body, where it taunted my pelvis. My mouth found its way to his sternum, which felt like a more neutral place, and I kissed him there passionately, sucking the skin, listening for his response, taming myself from eating him alive.

He lifted my head up and started kissing my mouth. We were both hungry for each other.

"I don't wanna go too fast for you," I said, between kisses.

"It's okay," he said, "I'm good. Right now, I just want you," he breathed, "I just want you right now."

I reached for his hips and clasped him tighter to me. I grabbed his ass and squeezed.

"I wanna leave my pants on," he said.

"Okay," I agreed, "pants on."

He gently pulled my arms off his ass and brought them behind my back, holding my wrists together while he licked my nipples and tugged at them with his teeth. It was divine. And of course it made me imagine him doing the same thing to my clit, which got me all kinds of aroused and way more wet. *Pants on*, I reminded myself.

"Max," I asked, "When you want me, does your cock get hard?"

"Yeah," he groaned, "my cock is so hard for you."

"Max," I panted between kisses, "I could suck your cock."

He paused.

"With your pants on," I added.

"Yeah?" he asked.

"Yes, Max," I stated, in a sultry voice. "I'm offering you a blow job. Do you want one?"

"Fuck," Max responded. "Yeah, just unbutton my fly and pull it out."

I wrapped my palms around Max's thighs and brought my mouth close to his crotch. I took a long breath in, inhaling him and his scent, and let a heavy breath leave my mouth with all the heat pressed against his pants, at the crotch and thigh, high up.

When I undid Max's fly, I imagined coaxing his cock out and how, once freed, it would spring to life in the little arena of this, his lap.

"Damn," I moaned, rubbing my face in his crotch. "What a fine cock you have."

I opened my mouth and looked up at Max with hungry eyes, lowered my hanging mouth toward his fly, and swallowed. Max whimpered. I moved my head slowly up and down, rhythmic, gripping Max's thighs. I moved my hand into his thigh crease so that the back of my knuckles would rub against his pubic bone as I encircled his shaft. My body started gyrating at the hips, I couldn't help it.

I was getting so turned on I wanted to jam my hand down my own pants while I sucked Max off, but I resisted and kept focused on the task at hand, to see if I could get Max to cum by blowing his etheric dick. His neck was ropy with tension, his cheeks flushed, his head tipped back. He looked like he was getting close.

I pulled my head up and wiped my mouth with the back of my hand. His eyes pleaded for more. I kept stroking Max through his pants, jacking off his cock. He started breathing really fast and short.

"Breathe," I instructed, thinking of how I like to be reminded of the same thing when I'm close to an orgasm. "Breathe deep all the way down your body through your pelvis to the tip of your cock."

Max altered his breath.

"I want you to keep breathing deep like that while I take your cock deeper into my mouth and pump it," I said firmly. While Max managed his breath and the build of his orgasm, I started moving my head again, while keeping my hand circling as before, both at once.

"Come with your pants on," I instructed as Max gasped and let loose between my arms. "Come all over my face," I demanded, as we both stifled the sounds of our ecstasy.

We were pouring forth and holding back, screaming as softly as we could manage.

Long-Haired Butch

SHE WAS MUCH older than me. The kind of longhaired butch I used to fantasize about as a teen: commanding, attentive, really good at reading the room, really good at reading women. There was just something about her. I was pulled into her field. She pulled up a stool and handed me a drink, inviting me to sit next to her. As she talked, elbow on the table, she flicked her hand in the air with a quick gesture, and I lost track of what she was saying—all I could imagine, like a flashback, was her hand in my pussy and my animal wail of pleasure. Can you have a flash-forward? Was I even thinking in linear time? It was just a fantasy. I shivered, taking a sip of my beer, tuning back in to listen to her, to suss out if she was even someone I wanted to share my body with. I don't get naked with just anyone.

Belly to belly, shirts bunched up around our necks. Kissing long and wet and probing, our tongues exploring the caverns of mouths, my fingers running through her hair. My hands settled, cupping her head in one palm, tipping her head back, my other hand tracing the dimple down her chin and trailing to her collarbone, tugging the ropy muscles of her neck, gripping the nape of her neck, thrusting our bodies together.

Her finger curled inside my asshole, her tongue on my clit. This jigsaw of us, how we fit just right.

She ended up being everything I ever wanted and more.

Long hikes through the woods, making love under waterfalls, and in lakes, and against the soft moss of the forest floor and the rough bark of unsuspecting trees.

She sang me love songs on the guitar, queering the lyrics so that I'd laugh and wouldn't go into a feminist rage over the patriarchal bullshit that ruined all the good old songs of the 70s. She took them back and made them even better.

We had a hot summer of lust and love and singing and swimming. What more could I have ever wanted at twenty-five? It didn't last. It didn't need to. A part of me will always love her for that time we spent, being real with each other, being generous. The lyrics are forever replaced in my head, and whenever those songs come on, I feel the weight of her breasts like ripe fruit against my belly, the curve of her inside me, the sun shining down like honey.

Bifurious

MY NEW BI boyfriend is cute and sexy and gay in all the ways that get me hot. He dresses in fancy crisp shirts and trim jeans that show off his tight little body that's all muscle. He laughs like a girl and drinks Manhattans with his pinky finger up. When a hot guy walks by, I watch my boyfriend's eyes follow the swing of his hips, the bounce of his ass. Then we wink at each other, nod, and giggle. My new bi boyfriend is such a doll. He doesn't feel threatened at all by my other lovers—not my girlfriend or my trans boi. (I have quite a collection.)

My new bi boyfriend is queer, and man alive, does he love pussy. I've never been with anyone who worshipped pussy like him. He is infatuated with it. He could lick, caress, rub, and fuck my pussy all day and never want to stop. He squirms just thinking about it, licking his lips and giving me a hungry stare. He's so sensual, using his hands and the touch of his skin all over my body. He stays turned on for hours, and he will put his lips on any part of my body and moan, all night long.

My new bi boyfriend is married. His wife is a hot piece of ass. I want her to be my best friend. And my lover. And my mother. And my sister. I want to lay in her arms. I want her to pet my hair. I want her to whip me and fuck me inside out with my own strap-on.

My new bi boyfriend and his wife have kids. They play outside in the sprinkler while the adults flirt like mad. We take vacations together. Once the kids go to sleep, we fuck like crazy. Me, my boyfriend, his wife, and her boyfriend. We are all terrifically hot for each other. And that's actually saying a lot. I'm not hot for just anyone. I just happened to have landed in an excellent situation.

I met them in a coffee shop. The three of them were there, no kids, and by the time my drink was up, all the chairs were taken. They invited me to join them in their booth. They hit on me. All three of them! All these toes touching mine under the table. I gave them my number, and the husband was the first to call.

He invited me on a date. We got drinks at the Fisherman's Tavern. We laughed all night long. I kept thinking I'd met him somewhere before. I kept thinking that somehow I'd known him my whole life.

We went on more dates. We had dinner. We saw a concert.

We played pool.

We were both so terrible at pool that the game lasted two hours. We just kept plunking the balls around the table with our cues, never getting them in the pockets. But we teased and flirted with each other, and that part held my interest. At one point the white ball was way in the middle of the table and I couldn't reach it. He asked if I needed help and I said no, I'd figure it out myself. He said he wanted to help. His hands twitched and I could read them—he wanted to put his hands around my waist, or on my thigh. He looked hopeful, earnest, turned on. I blushed and said no, I got it. I know how to play hard to get, at least a little, at first. I lay my body over the table in a suggestively contorted way. His pants shifted, I could see it. He had a glimmer in his eye.

He shut the door. There were lots of other rooms with pool tables in them. And it was a slow night. Maybe no one would come in.

He walked up to me and turned me so the small of my back was against the pool table. He took my cue and placed it against the wall. He turned his cue horizontal and pressed it against my wrists, my body. I bent back and he pinned me to the pool table. He bit my neck. He bit at my shirt. He pressed the cue harder into my arms, then moved it to my hip bones. He shifted so his crotch was touching my crotch. I could feel the hot beat of his cock through his pants. My pussy was getting all feverish and queasy. There was this spiraling ache going from my belly button down to my clit. He met my stare and whispered, "Is this what you want?"

I nodded my head. I arched my neck back. I opened my mouth and started panting. I licked the rim of my teeth with my tongue. He released me from under the pool cue, tossed it aside, and grabbed my waist and pulled me up.

I spun him around and pressed him to the wall. The wall was cold and flat, and I wanted his bare ass to feel that. I stripped his pants and underwear down and left them tight around his ankles. He pulled my shirt over my head and turned my neck hard to the side. He bit into the back of my neck and I screamed a little. Then he spun me around so my back was to the wall. The cold of it shocked me. I gave him a wicked little smile to indicate that, yes, this was just what I wanted. He thrust his knee between my legs and pushed down on my shoulders so that his thigh could touch my sex. I scooted forward to grind my pussy on his thigh. My panties were soaked.

I leaned forward and moaned in his ear. His earlobe was a little toy I played with using my tongue and teeth. When I lightly nibbled the crest of it, I felt his body release with a sigh. I breathed heavy and slow in his ear while he reached under my bra to toy with my nipples, making me groan. I reached under his shirt and rubbed his nipples too, with little circles of friction. His weight flattened me to the wall, and we began to grind crotch to crotch.

I pushed his hair back and pulled his lips away from mine so I could see his face, which was intense with longing. Pushing him towards a chair, I sat him down roughly, grabbed his jaw, and kissed him long and sloppy. I yanked the rest of our pants and underwear off and threw them in a tangled heap, grabbed a condom out of his back jeans pocket, ripped it open, and threw the wrapper on the ground.

His cock was hard and bobbing straight up, a little gleaming hint of cum at the tip. Holding the condom in my hand, I made it look like I was about to put it on. But I didn't. I hesitated and looked in his eyes. They were brimming with longing. His mouth opened. "Please."

I swooped down and swallowed his cock in my mouth, so suddenly he gasped. His cock shook in my mouth as he adjusted to my hot, wet hold on him. My fingertips lightly traced his belly button, the crease of his thighs, and around his balls. Scooting my hand under his butt, I felt his little puckered anus. As I licked and sucked his cock, my middle finger thumped his butthole. Boy, did he like that. I sincerely hoped no one would open the door.

His grunts were getting loud. "Shhh," I whispered, and I crammed my fingers into his mouth.

His body was writhing, but I didn't want him to come too fast. Slowing down, I got ready to put the condom on him, but he jumped up and spun me around and pushed me into the chair. He grabbed my shirt from the floor and tied my ankles to the chair with it. My lace bra stayed on, but he yanked it down to expose my breasts. I groaned and leaned my head back when he pinched my nipples lightly between his fingers. He sniffed my skin, my shoulders, my armpits, my belly—his mouth soft, his chin prickly, his tongue licking the creases of my thighs. I felt a long, warm exhale on my pussy, making my hairs stand on end.

Pulling back the lips of my pussy, he nosed at my clit. I started to squirm. I felt a cool whistle of air on the hood, and it stiffened immediately. My clit just got harder and more plump as he licked it up and down, up and down, lightly at first, but then with more pressure. When he could feel my muscles start to tense, he backed off to whisper-light, and licked me with the faintest pressure. My knees flopped open as if the springs holding me together had gone slack.

When he put his hands around each of my wrists and pressed them into the rail of the chair, the tingling in my pussy escalated up to my belly and shimmied down my thighs. My head started to float off my body like it was a bubble, and that's when I knew I was going to come in his mouth. He sensed it, and I knew he wanted me to, but he also wanted to fuck me in the poolroom. I, too, wanted to get fucked in the poolroom. And I didn't know how much time we had left before someone walked in and wrecked it for us.

"Stop," I said. "I wanna fuck."

I still had the condom in my hand. Spitting into my other hand, I rubbed it all over his hard cock, stretched the condom on, and rolled it down. He freed my ankles, pulled me up, and pressed me to him. Our bodies were a hot beating frenzy of desire.

His cock moved back and forth between my thighs, grazing my clit and driving me wild. My pussy hole was throbbing for him, and I couldn't wait to feel that plunge.

Without disentangling, we ambled to the pool table, where my hands landed on a pocket that I could grasp to steady myself. His cock was rubbing my pussy in little circles, which were getting wider as he started to enter me. The head circled inside me, and I felt my knees buckle. I could barely keep standing. He grabbed my ass and pinched his nails into my skin, which woke me up and got me ready to fuck furiously. I wanted him deep, so deep.

He grabbed my hip bones and, still circling, pressed into me. I let him go in, as far as he could, right away, and I felt an explosion of wetness erupt inside. A tingle zipped up the length of my cunt that blasted sparkles into my belly. His breathing got really heavy, then. I told him to fuck me hard and slap my ass, and he did exactly what I wanted. I was gasping at the strength of his body, the length of his cock, and I was smiling so big it hurt. The thrill was intense. *Pleasure pleasure pleasure* ran through my head like a banner. I could see my tits bouncing up and down with the thrusting of our bodies, and that got me even more excited.

The door started to creak open. He twisted his head, saw it, and quick as a flash stumbled both of our bodies over so we could press our weight against it. He was still inside me, and my pussy was starting to feel the hot swell of ecstasy building as I thought about the people who could have come in, and about my lover saving us so we didn't have to stop. There was just the thickness of the door between us and them.

He kept fucking me, staying deep and only thrusting a tiny bit, the tip of his cock rubbing my g-spot. The bone of his pelvis grinding my clit. I squeezed my cunt muscles and he moaned. I kept them squeezed as he thrust in and out, imagining my heart opening and melting into my cervix, imagining his heart opening and melting into the tip of his penis. I imagined that red swollen warmth of my cunt and his cock melding. Melting.

He twisted my nipples. I leaned forward to suck greedily on his neck and then moved my way up to his earlobe again. He made his movements subtle then, micro-fucking me deeper than deep. My body was so relaxed, I kept feeling more and more heavy as the strength of his arms held me up. He pressed his lips to my collarbone and began to suck.

His fucking got harder, but I could hardly feel it. My whole body was quivering in ecstasy. I went loose, held together by nothing but these arms, this bucking cock. His body started to tense, then relax. He changed his breath and let out a moan. I could feel the warm spray of his cum flooding the condom. My cunt reacted with a spasm of fluid. I went into convulsions of pleasure, over and over again. Like circles raining down.

The people on the other side of the door jiggled the handle. They pushed on the door. My lover pushed back on the door using my body weight and his, his palm on my breastbone, his eyes locked in mine with a knowing look of dreamy pleasure. He kept both his hands against the door and held it shut while I grabbed my clothes and got dressed. Then I handed him his clothes and took a turn pressing the door closed. With my back to the door, I buttoned his pants and adjusted his collar. I smiled. He smiled. He patted my hair smooth and fussed with my bangs before we stepped away from the door toward the pool table.

When the door opened, it revealed two fully clothed people kissing, just making out, in a room filled with the languid humidity of sex.

Then we went to his place, where his wife and her boyfriend were home playing cards, a bottle of bourbon between them with four glasses, and some sultry song crooning on the stereo. We walked in smelling like the spicy sweet aroma of sex. Their kids were already asleep. His wife and her lover perked up the moment we entered the house.

"Let me help you bathe," the wife said eagerly, grabbing my hand

and pulling me towards the bath. I knew she'd want to fuck me before she bathed me. The smell of her husband on me, our cum mixed together, would be irresistible to her. And, I thought, we should give the men some time to themselves.

Mythic Double-Pronged

WHEN I WAS just coming into the act of sexual fantasy, I stumbled upon a creature in my imagination that excited me deeply. In the scenario, I am sitting on a chair in my apartment doing something quiet and still, like reading or knitting or embroidery. The door blows open briefly and then shuts, containing a sense of privacy, and I can feel the invisible presence of something or someone mystical. Before my eyes, a god-like creature materializes. Part human, part beast, more spirit than anything, like a pictogram pulled off a cave wall and cast to life.

The soft and strong and delicate and noble being steps toward me on two human legs. The being's head and neck are somewhat animal, like an elegant elk, with simple antlers, but it has godly human eyes and a human mouth. Below the belt the creature is human, and springing forth from between its legs are two long, elegant, slim pricks. Look, I, like you, might appreciate some girth at times, but it is not the only way to go. There's something about a slender dick that really turns me on. More wiggle room, more flex and subtle motion. It's true what they say: it's not the size of the thing that matters but how you use it. But, here I am waxing on about dick size in the middle of whispering to you one of my most secret fantasies, and a bestial and double-donged one at that. So, let me interrupt myself once again to continue.

I was much younger when I invented this fantasy, and although I'd already experienced anal sex and enjoyed it, I associated it with muscle tension and a bit of pain at the time, so perhaps that was in the back of my consciousness when I imagined this creature with long, finger-like genitals that would eagerly penetrate both my holes at once. In the daydream, the beast comes towards me, curious, silent, breathtaking, and aroused with a demeanor that is gentle and inquisitive.

This is not a story in which I am taken like an animal. This is a graceful, gracious love scene in which we stare into the others' eyes, me and the spirit-beast, and we paw at each other in a make-out kind of way while the beast is still sort of invisible, or, rather, translucent, and not entirely there. I can feel and not feel this other being—both touching and being touched—so it's really energetic. It's like how I imagine sex scenes in the Greek myths when a god and a human lock bodies, translucent and feisty and full of cosmic eros. Where everyone is very much embodied and also very much etheric. Anyway, back to my god-fucking dream.

So, the spirit-beast and I are in it to win it. I hesitate to use he/him pronouns because the creature is so androgynous, equal parts masculine and feminine energies. They've got their wide, dark doe-eyes lowered to me, and I'm breathing in their breath, which smells like melted chocolate and fresh hay, and I reach out my fingers to their lithe smooth chest. And the two proboscis penises are these lively oddities, like something ancient and surreal come to modern life. I wriggle out of my panties and take off my clothes, and the beast nuzzles my body with tenderness, and I can both feel it really strongly but also barely feel it at all. The beast kneels and gently lifts me up. We are still gazing into each other's eyes. I feel their breath on my neck like the warmth of a horse's snuff. I'm crazy wet and so turned on—it's like nothing I've ever experienced. I mean, have you ever fucked a *god*?

And then the lights go out. At least that's what it feels like. The creature has slid into me. The room gets black and stars electrify the air and there's a swirling sparkling sensation that overcomes me. My pussy is rippling as if all the harmonic rhythms of the galaxy are playing my insides like a harp. I get sucked into the cosmos and I'm floating, and my mouth is open in an awestruck, blissed-out pleasure grin, and tears are squirting out of my eyes. It feels like my heart is shining like a torch, and all the walls I used to wear there have crumbled to dust, and in their place is a melty sensation that feels like being dripped inside out with molten honey.

It's the slitheriest, sexiest thing I've ever experienced. A part of me knows intellectually that I'm in the arms of the translucent mythic man-beast as his penises leap to life inside me, stretching lithely and arching and rhythmically moving, causing all kinds of immensely pleasurable sensations. But this other part of me isn't in my mind at all. I'm in some other place, I'm in my essence, at one with the cosmos.

I start to come. But it's not just any orgasm. It's like an endless unwrapping inside me, like a thousand orchids bursting into bloom, like a bushel of effervescent pomegranates getting cracked open and a zillion seeds popping open and juice splattering the clouds. My heart is brighter than the sun. And throughout my body, the moon wanes and waxes and tumbles around like a year on fast-forward, sliding with fullness and darkness and slivers of crescents and stars, and ohh—there are so many stars inside me.

After I come for the hundredth time, I fall instantly asleep, and when I wake, I see the man-beast roaming towards the door. Our eyes meet one more time and my entire body enlivens with celestial sparkles. I know the spirit-beast will always be a part of me after what we shared together. My pussy and asshole feel as if they are constructed of dazzling glitter and the magic dust of meteors, and I fall back asleep, and when I wake, I am forever fulfilled.

Flirting Softly

WE'D BEEN EYEING each other a lot and doing that thing where you lightly touch each other on the elbow and knee, and so I suspected we were heading for a kiss, but she was keeping some distance between us and so was I, neither of us willing to take the risk that might spoil our burgeoning friendship, so finally I just decided to be direct.

"Ameya," I said, and I looked into her eyes until the chattering energy between us ceased and the pause grew strangely long, "do you think we're heading for a fling?"

I watched her eyes startle and her lips curl, some heat steaming off her cheeks and neck—I could feel it. She glanced up at me, opened her lips, and quickly looked down again, laced her fingers together, cracked her knuckles, and asked, "Is that what you want?"

"Yes," I said.

I'd never been so direct before. It felt amazing. Either way I was in good standing with myself and that's what mattered. If she said no, I reasoned I had no cause to be embarrassed. I'd put my desires out there and been clear.

"Here's the thing," Ameya explained, "I'm just out of a relationship you know, and I don't know what I want right now, and I like you, and I don't want to hurt you. I have to be honest and question myself, do I just want the attention and the heat? Is it fair, if that's true?" Her sweater slipped off the edge of her shoulder, revealing her smooth skin.

In this moment, we were standing awkwardly on either side of my front door. I felt relieved she'd been so frank with me. Sharing some mutual attention and heat with no expectations sounded great to me. I smiled and pulled on the elbow of her sweater. "Do you want to come in and talk about it?" I asked, flirting softly.

"Yeah," Ameya nodded. Stepping behind her, I wrapped my arms around her and scooted us both into the house and we laughed.

"I don't have a plan or any set intentions. I just feel something, and it seems fun to explore it. I'm not gonna pin you down. Well. I mean . . ." I laughed, and so did she.

"OK," she said. "Yes." And I started to move toward her. "Wait—" she said, putting her finger up. "Now you know I want you, let's see how you go about it." And with that she took off, skipping off to my bedroom and through the back door to the yard. I felt a hot stone drop into my belly and my mouth began to water. Oh, shit. Ameya!

We played around in the backyard, chasing each other and flirting and laughing. She ran around and hid. I snuck around and tried to find her before she ran off. We played a little tag, our fingers brushing the other's skin in the speed of things. She had me chase her back into the house until she was in the corner of the living room. We were both panting. I stepped toward her, moving in. "Let's build a fire," she suggested.

While I was stacking wood and stuffing crumbled newspapers into the hearth, Ameya came up and stood behind me, her legs straddled, shins grazing my ass. She ran one finger down the back of my neck. I shivered. The fire was heating up now, warming my face, and Ameya kneeled down to blow into the flames with me. Her cheek was right beside mine in the orange glow. I felt my pussy clench in my pants. *Damn*, I thought, *what to do. Is it time to kiss her? Seems like she wants it to start slow, but she also asked me to go after her.*

Get out of your head, I reminded myself, *get into your body, your heart.* I took a deep breath and let my energy sink past my ribs and into my belly, settling into my hips. And then I looked at Ameya. She was doing that thing where she was looking at me with half-lowered lids, holding back a smile. Her eyelashes so long and beautiful, the deep brown luxury of her eyes, those cheekbones, her sweetness.

"Ameya," I whispered, "kiss you? Or wait?"

Her cheek came to mine, her lips brushed my jaw as she lifted them to my ear. "Wait." *Oh, yes*, I thought, *I will wait.*

My body softened into Ameya's slowness, and I could think of nothing else to do but just be with her. Our eyes met, and we didn't turn away. We got lost like that. I'd never really looked into anyone's eyes like that before. And it was just real. I wasn't guessing about love or the future or putting anything on it, I just was being there with her: we were just connected.

Time went by. I felt my body shift to a forest of falling leaves.

At some point Ameya held my hand. And then she was drawing me to her. We stayed like that for a while, our chests pressed together, and I could feel the beat of her body within mine. Her hand was on my back, her palm between my shoulder blades, our heads resting together. I felt her head turn and her breath against my neck. I dipped my head toward her neck and let my lips graze the soft skin from her collarbone up to her neck.

"You want me?" I asked softly.

"Yeah, I do," she said.

And I felt her fingers slide under my shirt. I moved my arms to her waist and tugged her belt loops, moaning that kind of moan when you're really turned on. She laughed. Her hands clutched my braids and tipped my head back like she was appraising me.

"Let's see what you like," she said slyly, taking me in, her eyes lit up by mystique and the glow of the fire. "You chased me around the garden," she murmured.

"Yeah," I said, "I guess I did."

"My turn now," she said playfully, taking me by the shoulders. "Can I pin you down? Just for tonight?" Her eyes were luscious and wet.

"You'd better do that," I answered.

And, oh, she did.

White Table

SHE WAS REMEMBERING his grip on her hand. A tight, dry grip that felt more like a press than a squeeze—sure, steady, a firm hold. With his fingers wrapped around her wrist like that, he was sending her body a message: stop, don't move, you are safe, you are held, you are desired. It was the memory of that grip on her wrist that brought her back to his apartment for the second time.

That's what got her to that place. Back to that living room with the sleek white table. And that's what got her to that place in her body— where a slow heat started its churn, a steam rising within her.

It was that feeling left in her wrist. A tingling, a longing. She could still feel the wrap of his fingers, as if they'd left a print, like the kind of photo paper you leave out in the sun with a leaf on it. After sunset when the leaf has blown away, the paper still holds its imprint, a tiny sketch whose shadow ran off. A memory of an afternoon in the sun made visible. How is it that after a week, she could still feel his touch vibrating in her skin? She inspected her wrist from all angles. It looked as it always did, delicate but strong, a graceful stretch of skin and muscle, able to twist and torque as it needed to. She didn't look any different, but she felt so changed.

This time there were no other people in his apartment, no clutter of heels and oxfords chattering the wood floor, no clink of ice cubes in cocktail glasses, no music parading through the stereo speakers. It was quiet and still, just the two of them.

The expectation between them was known. The message traveled between their lips, their eyes. He showed her the suitcase. She pointed to several items. He smiled and asked. She agreed. Her safeword was *Cherry*. She didn't need it. Not a word was spoken between them after that. But she had it. And she would not hesitate to use it if she needed to. It was like a keepsake in her pocket, a cold hard assurance that she had the key to the door of her safety.

She had been thinking about that sleek white coffee-table. The way it floated a little above the geometry of the rug. How it had looked so impeccably clean.

Ever since the party, and his grip, she'd thought of his sweet smile that she had intuitively trusted, the mix of his gentle kindness and the firmness of his grip—it was not a squeeze, not at all, there was no neediness, not a hint of desperation, just a hold, a full circle of fingers against her skin. She wanted that grip on her ankles, on her thighs. She wanted the cool, clean white coffee-table flat to her skin. She had imagined it many times.

She had envisioned her naked body on the cold surface of the table, her breasts and belly pressed flat to it, her wrists and ankles cuffed together above the small of her back, her head to the side, mouth gagged, eyes blindfolded. Waiting. How he'd make her wait for him. And then she'd feel his shadow on her skin.

She'd sense him reading her. He'd trickle the whip lightly along her spine. One hundred times.

Gauging her energy. Assessing the subtle arch of her back, the level of her readiness, her yearning. He'd be able to tell where she was blocked, and at one hundred and one she'd feel the sting of the whip in exactly the spot she needed it. Her ass, her thigh, her back, he'd know. She would wait for it, and then she would be given the release. The smack, the hot burst, the tingle and zip, like lightning under her skin. She'd feel it like a small electrocution. And then he would reassess her and determine what she needed next.

In her fantasy, she'd feel the churning twist of his thick cock screwing into her pussy, slowly at first, probing, exploring. Imploring. He'd want to learn her, he'd want to master her.

It didn't happen exactly as she had fantasized. Of course it didn't. But the thrill of the actual experience overturned the script she had played out in her head.

She was right about the white table; there was something special about it. Hidden underneath the edge were steel clasps. She couldn't see them, but she could hear them click into the puffy black leather cuffs that gripped her wrists and ankles. She was splayed naked and face-up on the table, her arms and legs bent and held to its cool curve. A blindfold tied around her head. She felt his fingertips running down the cleft of her chest, the curves of her ribs, brushing light circles around her navel, as if he were collecting the measurements of all the ridges of her body with his fingertips, these warm and gentle instruments. And then she felt that grip, the grip she was waiting for, a warm clutch on her thigh. He held her firmly, and still. Just that same way. He held her thigh with one hand and she could feel him watching her while she lay there, just barely breathing.

He held his other palm flat just over her belly. Just below the place where her ribs branched into a graceful archway and spread like the fingers of open palms. His hand hovered above the hollow above her navel. She could feel the dry warmth of electricity in that tiny layer of air, the air between bodies. She wanted to feel his touch, so she pressed her belly up to meet him. His hand must have slightly backed away. She took a deeper breath and let her belly expand. There! She touched him. He let her. She took another deep breath, again seeking the warmth of his hand. Ah, there it was, his palm, stretched flat, hovering just above her. He let her develop a rhythm of breathing, so that she touched him with each inhale.

She was breathing deeply now, and it was sending energy throughout her body. A new vibrancy was growing within her. She felt the warm shadow of his hand move down her body a little lower. His hand was instructing her to breathe deeper, lower. She followed his guidance, directing her breath lower into her pelvis. And then he touched her, ever so lightly with his finger, one small spot on the mound of her pussy, under the curl of hairs, above her pubic bone. He wanted her breath to go right there.

She let the growing heat and pulse of her pussy draw her breath to it like a magnet. The energy was building. Her lips were gaining heat, getting plumper, a buzz was circling her cleft. Deep in her pelvis she felt an aching sensation, a hard tug. And then a sudden smack hit her pussy lips, sending a bolt of light into her clit. It startled her body, sending shock waves roiling through her like grafts of light. She imagined her pussy at the helm of all that light, like a golden creature gleaming.

Moving her hips toward him was difficult. She was strapped so tightly to the table. She imagined how she'd look from above in a painting she might paint later. The shape of a body stretched and bent around that negative space. The warm luster of her skin in contrast to the shiny white table. Her nipples riding high on her flat, stretched breasts. Her legs splayed open like a house dog. Her cleft open, pulsing like a neon sign, liquid gold dripping from her pussy lips. She'd make them look raw, gorgeous, edible, irresistible. A thought drifted through her mind, that one of the gifts she was receiving from this man was a new perspective, to see herself as irresistible.

What came next was a new kind of glory. A strange mix of pain and pleasure that left her breathless and floating, yet acutely aware of every cell vibrating in her body. Every time he gifted her the pain she sought, she got that blast of pleasure that lifted upwards from the anchor of his steady grip.

Safe. Safely held. Safe because he watched her and read her right and wanted her to feel it all. She knew she was safe in the palm of his hand. Safe to be open, safe to be splayed. Safe enough to let go and float. She had found again something wild within her, something that came untamed.

Later, when she was on all fours, chained to the table, her head bridled and pulled back, a bit clamped in her mouth, and he was riding her, his cock thick and throbbing so full within her asshole, she couldn't even feel it all, all she could feel was the ecstasy of soaring and his firm grip on her left shoulder. Her nipples were pinched and chained tight to her wrists, and there were needles pinned behind her shoulder blades. She saw a version of herself sprouting wings and hurtling through the deep blue square of the skylight, set free into the night, into the starry unknown, into a blissful bodiless flight. She was more alive than she had ever been.

She left exactly the way she came, clean and dressed and brightly smiling, but with a slightly different smile—satiated, rather than expectant. The room, when she left it, looked the same, save for a small puddle glinting on the white table along with a few spatters of blood. A print that he would easily wash away, unlike the memory that stayed in her mind of an afternoon on the white table, and the new drawing of herself that surfaced within her body like a victory.

Soccer Game

I HAVE A thing for soccer players. I like them short and lean and full of muscle, all sweaty-headed and fierce. Soccer guys are spry and quick, with serious stamina and determination. They persevere. I like them with their heads shaved on the edges and a flop of curls up top, dripping with sweat. I like the way they eye the goal. I want them. Not just one. I want the whole team.

First, I want to make them earn it. They have to split up and wrestle each other while I watch and touch myself. Half the team shirts, the other half skins. Everyone in those tight silky shorts that highlight their ass muscles. When you make out with a player in those shorts, you can feel everything.

Line up, fellows! They get to lick my pussy one at a time. They can take up to forty-five seconds or so, nobody gets to hog me, and I rank them on their pleasuring skills. The ones who excel get to share their insights with the ones who need some lessons, but not through words, they mimic sucking my cunt on the other guy's nipple or on the head of his cock, dealer's choice. It should be said that any of them can *of course* opt out, and any of them who want to fuck each other instead can please do just that, in the wet grass and mud, right over there, where I can watch.

The rest of the team, up for a gang-bang, strips, and they hose each other down with warm water from the nearby hot springs. Come on, you guys, why not? One at a time, step right up and lick me, slick up your cock, and plunge in. I want to try you all on for size. Those shapely pecs, those ripped abs, thighs like hulky flying buttresses of muscle and brawn. Every kind of cock you could imagine.

Next time, though, it will be the women's team. Those slick, sweaty, thick lady thighs drive me even more wild. Naturally, we'd have an orgy. Or two. Offense watches defense orgy and then vice-versa. Once everyone's sweaty and muddy and tussled and the whole team is freshly fucked, they'll all line up and relay their favorite moments and their requests for the next sex-scrimmage. I'll take coach's notes to determine who gets to fuck who in the next game. At practice, we'll strip down to come up with some irresistible tactics for the playoffs.

An Added Thrill

FOR SHANNON'S FIFTIETH birthday, she requested a surprise sexual adventure. Leigh was nervous but determined to oblige, unsure what exactly Shannon had in mind. Did she want to try something new in bed, go to a sex club, or include someone else? Leigh always had trouble making decisions on her own, and Shannon was out of the race, so to speak, having asked for a surprise.

First, Leigh tried to think of what she could do on her own. Recreating their first encounter on a canoe seemed a bit too complicated. They no longer had the youthful bodies that could sidle up without capsizing a vessel. Did Shannon want this new outlandish encounter to occur just between the two of them? How was Leigh to intuit what Shannon was missing and suddenly be able to provide? That felt like a tall order. If there was some sex act she wanted from Leigh alone, she would have asked. So, late one night Leigh opened a dating app account on her cell phone, while Shannon snored by her hip, their kids tucked in bed down the hall.

Should she get a third or another couple? And what gender? She knew Shannon was open. They both were. After the debauchery they'd shared as college girls at camp all those summers, they'd each had a few dudes here and there throughout their twenties before they got back together. Many times over the last fifteen years, while fooling around with silicone dildos, they had lamented the absence of a warm, vivacious dick. "But the guy comes with it," they'd both groaned, cracking each other up. Maybe this was what Shannon wanted: a hot, live cock. No conversation, no intimacy, just a chance to play, a boytoy.

Leigh was flicking through candidates. No, no, no, maybe, hmmm. Would Shannon want someone based on looks, political views, intellect, physique? So hard to guess. She closed her eyes and imagined having a conversation with Shannon about it. *Tell me what you want,* Leigh begged in the dark, to the vision of Shannon's delighted face, spilling her sexual secrets, like a mirage floating over Shannon's sleeping form.

It came to her then. Leigh distinctly saw Shannon's face replaced with Benicio del Toro. Of course! Shannon had a huge crush on him. That would sharpen the focus of her search. Tall, golden, cut like a side of beef, thick eyebrows, pretty eyes, full lips. Okay, okay, now she was getting somewhere. Was Shannon hot for guys with sexy accents? Leigh wasn't sure. Was the thick head of hair important? Hard to say.

Just Benicio, or a woman too? She had a hunch that a third cis-woman was not what Shannon had in mind. The idea of a sultry hunk coming to fuck them both suddenly sounded deliriously delicious to Leigh, and she felt like she was getting a green light on her intuition as to what Shannon wanted. Full steam ahead. She kept scrolling, this time with more enthusiasm. No, no, no, maybe, yes. Maybe, no, yes, YES. After about a dozen yeses, Leigh set her phone down and settled into bed, relieved to have leapt over the first hurdle of Shannon's birthday preparations, and titillated by her own naughtiness.

That night, Leigh dreamed that a hunky Neanderthal came out of a cave and sauntered up to her, smelling like leather and musk. She could see a large hard bulge under his loincloth. The man stood in front of her, brawny muscles gleaming in the sun, and they silently communicated with their eyes. Around them, wild animals leapt and ran and hunted each other in a prehistoric landscape. Cheetahs tore apart a wildebeest. Lions gutted a giraffe. Hooves thundered by in packs, and there were snorts and rears and gnashing sounds. Leigh held the man's gaze until she heard his voice levitate above the fray.

What do you need? the man asked her, without moving his lips.

Dream Leigh said, "*I need to tell you that I don't know how to do this.*"

The man turned his head toward the chaos and blood spill.

Does the wild animal know how to gnash his prey?

Leigh nodded her head.

Dream man spoke with his eyes again. *He kills on instinct.*

"'*They*,'" Leigh corrected, out of habit. "We can't assume . . ."

Dream man put a finger to her lips.

You know how, he said. *Like this.* He gripped her elbows and pulled her toward him.

Suddenly Leigh was naked, her tits bobbing like apples, the Neanderthal's beefy hands around her waist. His cock enlarged comically like it was being pumped by a machine, and he slipped it into her like a thick log greased in butter. She moaned. She rode that cock like it was Shannon's whole hand.

But, actually, she was humping Shannon's ass in bed.

"Whoa, babe, what's got into you?" Shannon mumbled, waking to Leigh's thrusts coming at her like a hot boner. Leigh was half-asleep, still unaware that the dream was entirely a dream.

"You need a quickie before we get the kids up, honey?" Shannon purred, flipping around and slipping her hand into Leigh's pajama bottoms. Leigh awoke to Shannon fucking her with three fingers while kissing her neck.

"Slip your pinky up my ass!" Leigh ordered between gasps. She came like a bucking bronco. Shannon laughed, pleased by the surprise. She smacked her on the thigh and told her to get up and dressed, they'd be late for work and school.

The morning was a whirl. Leigh kept feeling the caveman's phantom cock inside her and flushing at her desk. *You know what to do,* he'd said. On her lunch break, Leigh remembered the app, logged on, and found quite a few messages. One of the hunky guys offered to bring his girlfriend. Another seemed sweet and unassuming. One sent a pic of his six-pack and ginormous biceps. And then there was Derek. *I'm a personal trainer,* he wrote. *Just looking for fun, nothing serious. I reallly like sex. Always wanted to be with a couple like you two.*

Her heart started beating audibly and her armpits burst with sweat. This guy was ripped. He was tall, dark, and handsome. He used three l's in "reallly." Was that a secret signal that means he knows his way around a clit? Would Shannon be into this guy coming over and banging them? She asked imaginary Shannon. The answer tumbled out before she'd even phrased the sentence. *Yes. Definitely yes. Message him back.*

The Saturday that was Shannon's birthday, the kids got up early and, whispering the whole time, made pancakes and coffee and chopped up fruit, and carried it all on a tray into the bedroom, singing happy birthday. Shannon roused, delighted, and they all ate, and then Leigh sent the kids out to clean up the kitchen. She handed Shannon her birthday present. The card read, "I love you, babe. Let's have some fun and start the next fifty years together with a bang." Under the tissue paper was a vintage motel key Leigh had picked up at an antique store and an artisanal sausage from the local butcher.

"Thanks, sweetie," Shannon said slowly, looking at her quizzically.

Leigh returned her look with a flirty smile.

Shannon turned the key over in her hand. "Am I missing something?" she asked.

"We have a date at a hotel later," Leigh informed her.

Shannon's eyes began to sparkle. "And the sausage?" she asked.

"You don't sense the symbolism there?" Leigh teased.

Shannon twirled the sausage like a baton.

"Sit on it," Leigh said, with a wink, and she left Shannon to mull it over.

***

Leigh had it all worked out. The kids would spend the day with Grandma at a theme park so they'd be gone a long, long time. Leigh had booked a king-sized room at the local boutique hotel and she'd given Derek, the boytoy, the room number and the time to arrive. Leigh's mother was under the impression they had a fancy lunch date and tickets to the opera's current matinee, so to her they were officially unavailable.

She got Shannon to the hotel early so that she could tell her the plan and check to see if it was what she wanted. If not, she'd call it off with Derek and have a sexy afternoon with Shannon all to herself. She had brought a playlist of some of their favorite songs from the early 2000s when they re-fell in love, massage oil, a bottle of whiskey, a few just-in-case dildos, their old vibrator, and a new kind of vibrator that looked like a microphone. She also had a box of condoms and a tube of water-based lube. She'd dropped some cash at the feminist sex shop, prepared for either scenario.

Leigh walked Shannon into the hotel on her arm. They checked in giggling, and they made out in the elevator on the way up. "Happy birthday, baby," Leigh said, as she gestured to the room and opened the suitcase full of sex toys and romance.

"Aren't you sweet," Shannon murmured, kissing her. "This is a real treat."

"Well, you have the option of an additional treat if you want it," Leigh said coyly.

"Oh?"

Leigh pulled out her phone. "This is Derek."

Shannon's eyes popped. "Oh."

"Yep. He will come over and fuck you in front of me, or fuck us both, or watch us fuck, whatever you want. If you want that."

"Wow," said Shannon. "I'm impressed."

"Thus, the sausage in your present."

"Ohhh." Shannon laughed. "My wife must really love me," she said, drawing Leigh in.

Leigh couldn't help but remember the caveman from her dream. He had pulled her in like that. She got wet.

"But," Leigh added, "if you prefer for this to be just us, I'll call it off with Derek. It's whatever you want, babe."

"Do we have time for you to wax my asshole?" Shannon asked.

"Nope," Leigh said.

"Ah, well. Fuck it." Shannon laughed. "Let's do this thing!"

"If I can handle your furry taint, so can Derek," Leigh asserted, teasing.

"Good point," Shannon said. "Weird that I felt self-conscious about it in front of a stranger. But I can embrace it."

"Let's embrace it all," Leigh whispered in her ear.

Shannon pulled Leigh to the bed. "You are so good to me."

***

Derek arrived on time, looking buff and freshly clean in a very tight T-shirt and Euro jeans. Leigh had messaged with him pretty extensively, to explain that it was a birthday present and a surprise, and that she had to get Shannon's consent first, and also to find out if he'd be cool with just watching as an alternative to an active threesome. She found him really agreeable and flexible, and was happy that he said he'd be open to whatever felt right. The whole thing felt surreal. Here they were. Now what?

They had not come up with a plan. When Derek knocked and then walked in, Shannon just burst into nervous laughter. "This is so cool you came here," she kept saying awkwardly, introducing herself more than once. Then she looked to Leigh, a little panicked.

Leigh cracked open the whiskey and offered Derek and Shannon a glass. She had to scurry into the bathroom to find a third glass, and took the opportunity to pee. While peeling the plastic off the cup, she tried to figure out how to get this thing going, but when she came out, Shannon had already gotten to second base with Derek, whose shirt was off, his pecs flexing under her hands. Leigh watched Derek lifted Shannon's shirt off and her breath caught with a pang of jealously. Frozen, she watched his hands, like softball mitts, caress Shannon's tits. She did have great tits. Leigh was accidentally gaping, unsure how she felt or what to do. Shannon sensed it and held out her hand, inviting Leigh in and kissing her deeply. Derek massaged Leigh's ass and then ran his fingers along her waist to Shannon's, creating a Leigh sandwich.

They all made out for a while, dropping one at a time every piece of clothing from the three of them. Limbs akimbo, three thatches of pubic hair, four tits, two pussies, one cock.

Leigh was the first to get on her knees. She spread Shannon's legs apart and pressed her feet to the floor, while Derek was grinding against Shannon from behind and holding her breasts. Leigh kissed Shannon's ankles, knees, and thighs. Shannon shivered at the sensation of Leigh's tits sliding up her shins, following the line of kisses.

Leigh paused to look up at Shannon with questioning eyes, as if to ask, *how is this threesome thing going for you, is it what you want?* Shannon nodded eagerly. Leigh chuckled, feeling very pleased with herself for making Shannon's fiftieth so special and memorable. She felt her heart swell. She grabbed ahold of Shannon's clit with her mouth and felt it, too, swell between her lips. While Derek and Shannon kissed and groped, Leigh made her soft tongue hard for a moment to run it from her wife's clit down to her taint in one swift, slick line. Shannon gasped.

I want Derek to enter her from behind, Leigh thought, *while she sits on my face.* She felt her clit tighten and upturn like a tiny boner. *But first, I wanna do a few other things.* Her imagination unleashed, Leigh grabbed Shannon's ass and steered her to the bed, where she slid onto her back and pulled Shannon's knees to straddle her hips. She moved Shannon's hips down to hers so that Shannon's clit was riding Leigh's. They both moaned as their clits rubbed and slid down the other's pussy lips, back and forth with Shannon's rocking. It was an added thrill to have Derek in the room watching them fuck like this.

Derek was standing off to the side, slowly pumping his cock, his mouth agape. Leigh commanded Shannon's hips to the rhythm of her choosing, the fluids slicking the double rungs of their gears. The heat was building between them with all the friction. Their clits were both engorged and getting bigger. Shannon was getting so excited so fast, Leigh decided to abruptly switch it up.

"Hey, babe," she asked Shannon between heavy breaths, "you wanna taste that sausage now?"

"Yes, please," Shannon whispered.

"Derek," Leigh asked, "you want a blow job from Shannon?"

Derek came trotting over to the other side of the bed and stood at its edge while they scooched into a new arrangement: Shannon on all fours, Leigh underneath her, Shannon's face pointed at Derek's crotch, his stiff, thick dick bobbing in the space between them. Shannon's gorgeously full tits were dangling over Leigh's face. Leigh nuzzled them, running butterfly kisses and soft lips over her areolas. Shannon loved that.

Shannon looked down and said, "I love you, baby. Thank you for this." Leigh heard Derek moan as Shannon took him into her mouth.

Wouldn't it be nice to give him a treat?, Leigh thought while sucking on one of Shannon's nipples. *He's a really sweet guy and so cute.* After sucking Shannon's other nipple, Leigh tensed her abs, backed her head off the edge of bed, and slid her tongue to Derek's taint, licking each ball, so that he arched his back and stuffed his cock deeper into Shannon's hungry mouth. Two mouths at once for Derek's cock and balls. That felt like a triumph! Especially for two chicks who preferred pussy to dick. Leigh had a brief flash-forward of them spilling this story to their best friends over a bottle of wine on the patio some late night and totally scandalizing everyone with their audacity.

Shannon had bragged about her oral sex skills with a dick, and Leigh had always assumed she was exaggerating, but listening to Derek's reaction, she realized Shannon was as skilled as advertised. Made sense. Shannon was amazing at giving head. She knew just what to do to get Leigh to the next level, building up slowly until she avalanched into her orgasm. And usually then another and another.

"Oh gawd, oh gawd," Derek was trilling. *We gotta make him last longer*, she thought. Leigh let Derek's balls loose and slid down the bed.

She had her eye on the prize: Shannon's hard, shiny clit.

As usual, Shannon read her mind. "Do you want to fuck me from behind, Derek, while my wife sucks me off?" she asked.

Leigh soon found herself underneath Shannon and Derek, who were on their knees. Her mouth grasped Shannon's pussy, her tongue flicking back and forth over Shannon's clit while Derek thrust his hips into Shannon, his cock pumping in and out of her pussy, which was dripping cum all over Leigh's face. Shannon was grunting and suppressing her howls, her breasts jostling like jelly. Leigh could smell everyone's sweat, and the pheromones were driving her wild. She unlocked her lips from Shannon's pussy and slid up to kiss her. She loved making Shannon taste her own cum between their lips, and she slid her tongue into Shannon's mouth in a way as to remind her, *this tongue just licked your clit like this.* They rocked back and forth together with the fucking. Shannon moaned into Leigh's mouth.

"This is so fun," she said, almost indecipherably.

"I want him to fuck me too," Leigh said. "Is that okay with you?"

"Yes, baby, yes, that's hot," Shannon mumbled between groans.

"But first . . ." Leigh said as she slid up the bed, "do that dolphin pose from yoga class."

"You mean the puppy pose," Shannon corrected her between thrusts.

"I thought it was a dolphin. The elbows thing." Leigh watched Shannon lower her elbows to the bed and press her chest to the bedsheets, her ass sticking up in the air. She could see Derek's meaty hands holding Shannon's hips while he pounded her from behind. Leigh now lay on the bed on her back and pressed Shannon's head down into her pussy, holding it there amidst the thrusts.

"Make me come," she instructed.

Shannon sort of nodded, her mouth full of pussy, her cunt full of cock.

The impact of each thrust rubbed Shannon's chin against Leigh's vulva in the most thrilling way. She was getting Shannon's tongue and lips and the power of each of Derek's whams. She could easily imagine how swollen Shannon's g-spot was right now. She always got that way with deep, hard fucking. That's why she loved it so much when Leigh wore a cock and bent her over the bed or pressed her hands to the wall of the shower and pulled her hips out, slipping her silicone in. She came best when fucked hard.

She knew by the sounds of Shannon's muffled wailing and the feeling of her own clit on the verge of explosion that Shannon was close. Leigh's climax was building, filling her whole pelvis with effervescence. It felt like a tiny electric hula-hoop was spinning in her clit, and she thought of a little demi-god DJ in there spinning records at a party. *What the fuck*, she started to question, before the orgasm overtook her like a tidal wave and she forgot everything else. Shannon's climax hovered around her—the echoes of Shannon's expletives as her mouth unlocked from Leigh's cunt, her tits thwapping wildly.

***

Shannon knew that Leigh loved to get fucked after a clitoral orgasm.

So, she was wasn't surprised when Leigh called, "Derek? Will you alternate fucking us?" After the muffled conversation in the middle of sex when they'd agreed it was time for them both to take Derek's cock, Shannon was glad to hear Leigh voicing her desires.

"Um, yeah," Derek, grunted. "Taking turns?"

"Yes!" they both said at the same time.

Derek slid his condom off and went to the bathroom to wash. Shannon's body had collapsed onto Leigh's. Her pussy felt so open and satiated at the same time, and still she wanted more. Leigh ran her hands over her and grabbed her ass, while Shannon, languid, lay cunt to cunt on top of her wife.

***

Derek, freshly washed, leaned down to swirl his tongue around Leigh's pussy. He sucked her pussy lips into his mouth and held her clit lightly between his teeth, putting pressure low down on the root. Leigh suppressed a shriek. She'd never had her pussy held captive in a man's teeth like that. It felt exhilarating. He hadn't gone down on Shannon yet. But if he did, she'd have to ask Shannon what she thought of this maneuver. Derek did some other moves down there, running his tongue inside her pussy. Leigh was feeling really ready for that D.

"I want you inside me," she moaned.

Derek stood up and held his cock in his hand. He placed one hand on Shannon's ass cheek and slowly inserted his cock into Leigh's pussy, one tiny bit at a time, twisting his cock a little bit each time.

"F-u-u-u-u-ck," Leigh wailed.

****

Shannon had her head pressed to Leigh's cheek, her body heavy and limp atop her wife, her pussy so close to Leigh's that she could feel each thunk electrify her. Leigh's whole body was taking a blissful throttle, while Shannon got the lustiest compersion she'd ever felt. She wanted the cock to switch pussies and enter her, but she didn't want Leigh to stop getting fucked. She could tell by the sounds Leigh was making that Derek was now using one hand to arouse Leigh further while he fucked her. Fifteen years and you know the sound of a thumb on your wife's clit.

"Okay, Leigh," Derek said, "Shannon's turn. Ready, Shannon?" and he slipped his cock out of Leigh and thrust it into Shannon. Leigh gasped as Shannon began panting.

"Oh, oh, ohhhhhh," Shannon sobbed, loving it.

Leigh was humping Shannon so hard in the absence of that cock. Derek switched again, driving them wild. Now he was in Leigh, and Shannon was craving the cock and turned on beyond measure, knowing that Leigh was getting fucked beneath her.

***

Derek was getting so worked up too that he could barely contain himself. He came in the condom, bucking hard into one pussy, or the other, he could no longer tell who was who, he was in such an altered state of wantonness.

"Will you grab those cocks?" one of the women asked, assuming he didn't need a breather.

There were two clean dildos sitting on the nightstand like raunchy bookends.

Derek grabbed the silicone cocks, lubed them up, and slipped one into each woman. He was glad to give his dick a rest for a moment and focus on the task of satisfying both women at once. Fucking them each with a dildo was like a new kind of interval training. He could feel it in his biceps, scalenes, and pecs. Although this was unlike any workout he'd ever done. Derek shook himself out of gym mode and zeroed in on the scene before him.

The dildos smacked as he plunged them in and out in sync. Leigh and Shannon suppressed screams and wild animal sounds, they pulled the others' hair, they gripped the bedsheets ferociously. Derek worked his body like the gym rat he was, sweat trickling down his chest. Both women came hard and then again and again. They smashed their hips together.

"Okay, okay," one of them announced, indicating it was enough for now.

Derek asked if they both wanted to rest and when they affirmed, he removed the cocks and laughed, seeing them roll over, sweaty and hot and covered in cum, their faces awash with glee and disbelief.

***

All three of them lay down, drank some whisky and water, and stared into space. Occasionally, one of them would burst forth with a giggle and the others would chuckle. Leigh absently reached for the vibrator and asked Derek and Shannon if they had it in them for a few more rounds. They both did. Leigh wanted Derek to go down on Shannon while she watched and jacked off, and everyone liked that idea, so she watched Derek lower himself to Shannon's pussy, and studied Shannon's face.

"Oh my god," Shannon exclaimed.

"Right??" Leigh affirmed.

Derek worked Shannon's pussy until she came, and Leigh was so turned on by the sight and sounds and smells, and the squinched-eyed and openmouthed expressions on Shannon's face, and feeling the vibrator buzz snaking all the way to her g-spot, she came hard, pitching her hips into the air, the vibrator whizzing against her clit.

Next, Leigh was in tabletop yoga position, her pussy spread wide, which she imagined looked like a gleaming oyster covered in briney cum froth, her clit all pearly. Shannon moved in to take the whole thing into her mouth, swallowing the cum and encircling Leigh's entire labia. Leigh pressed her hips back to make harder contact with Shannon's face and ground her hips, mashing her pussy in Shannon's mouth. At the same time, Leigh was sucking Derek's cock. It felt so good to command a man for a minute, she thought. She felt sensual, emboldened, artful, as she designed her movements and pressure to get Derek's cock to blow. Shannon's mouth was doing similar maneuvers to her pussy.

Leigh extracted the cock so she could talk. "Babe, will you lick my ass while I make him come?" she asked, and immediately Derek's breath caught. Shannon switched holes and began to ring Leigh's asshole with the tip of her tongue. Once she got it slick, she just kept rimming circles, making Leigh keen, strange sounds, while her mouth was stuffed with cock. Shannon slipped two fingers in. She knew what Leigh liked.

Derek, meanwhile, was stifling a howl and rocking tiny thrusts into her mouth. Leigh knew her tongue was giving Derek's penis a rapturous rub. She could hear his climax building to the point that he squawked. He withdrew, and she felt a sudden splat on her back. Derek ran to get a towel to mop it up, whispering *holy shits* of appreciation.

***

Derek needed a break, but Leigh and Shannon weren't done yet.

"Climb on top of me," Shannon said, and Leigh hefted herself to straddle her wife. Pussy to pussy, they began to rock again, but this time with a vibrator at the nexus of their clits. "Ohhh!" They were moaning, rubbing each other, and writhing while the microphone-shaped toy buzzed. From the chair in the corner of the hotel room, Derek was twisting his own nipple and fondling his balls.

Leigh and Shannon came at the exact same time, a chorus of grunts, groans, and profanities, which reminded Shannon of the early days at Campfire Night, when they'd fingered each other and humped thighs until they came in tandem and collapsed on the grass, naked and sweaty, smelling the fresh summer air under the dark sky, looking up all dreamy-eyed at the bright stars. Everything felt magical then. As it did now.

Here she was turning fifty, and Shannon had her whole life ahead of her, the better half of her life, when she knew herself, owned her pleasure, was bold enough to ask for what she wanted, and didn't have all the emotional obstacles in the way of getting her needs met, like she did as a young woman. *This is the start of adventure*, she thought, covered in sweat and cum and the scent of her wife's cunt. This is the life I want.

***

Leigh was also thinking back to the young love they'd shared at twenty, how she'd cherished Shannon so much it made her heart ache then, and how she felt that way again now. They were a family, they had these gorgeous kids, and as they aged, they might be losing some of the youthfulness from their skin and gaining a bit around the waist, but they were so much more comfortable in their bodies and with each other.

The way that Shannon could ask for an adventure and Leigh could provide it, with this crazy vortex of afternoon smut, with this guy, made Leigh love her partner even more. They were in this life together, for better and for worse, for the daily grind of work and home and for the occasional outrageous grind of a mini-orgy. Leigh felt so lucky, so in love. Only a few months until her fiftieth. Maybe they could do this again. Maybe Derek would bring a friend?

Slow Burn on the Beach

REMEMBER THAT TIME on the beach? We'd known each other about a year or so. During that time our eyes had deepened when we looked at each other and I got shivers up my spine when you came close. But neither of us had ever made a move. Afraid to spoil what we had. Afraid it'd mean we couldn't be friends.

We were up on the cliffs watching a seagull flit across the sound until we couldn't see it anymore, it just became a speck in all that blue, and I asked, "Where'd it go? Can you see it?" And you said you'd lost sight of it too. And I raised the question, "What if it just got too tired and gave up and sank into the sea with one final shrug?" And you said you were wondering the same thing. "How far is too far for a seagull?"

How long is too long for us?

I'm the nerd in the dimly lit bar writing you covert love letters on my computer, which I'll probably never send, while I sip my bourbon. Dido is playing through the speakers and it takes me back to the 90s when we were acquaintances and I always thought you were cute, and right now I think I'd like to lay my head against your shoulder in front of a fire somewhere. Supposedly, I'm just emailing you to "check in" and see how you're doing, but really I'm wondering what your neck smells like and if you'd ever go for someone like me.

I remember earlier that day on the beach, we'd gone swimming and splashed in the waves, both of us in our suits looking fine. The sun was bright and the breeze was strong and salty. We had an excellent view of three women and a man sitting on a blanket. The women were in bikinis, their legs bare and their hair blowing in the breeze. And we were joking about their love life behind doors, as if they were always having orgies when they weren't at the beach. You scripted that the thin, muscled woman and the punk, elfin woman met up after these group beach ventures in a secret sandy hidey-hole where it was *on*. I added that the man was a prominent activist-revolutionary and the woman in the yellow bikini was a girl-next-door type who had a thing for boss babes. The possibilities were endless. We invented more and more of these seaside trysts that others had in a fantasy, which we were excluded from, while we lay there, the heat building on our skin and under our skin. It was building under mine. Was it under yours too?

I told you about the 1920s French artists I'd been researching and how looking at pictures of Lee Miller, Dora Maar, Ady Fidelin, and Nusch Éluard made my insides uncoil with a pleasurable plunk and I'd instantly get wet. "It's like I both want to *be* them *and* fuck them," I told you. *I want to receive penetration and give it,* I thought, but I kept that to myself. *I want to lick the salt off everyone's supple body,* I mused, silently. "I want to suck on the treasures of each of them," I mumbled. You had nothing to say then. You just giggled, raised your eyebrows, and smiled at me, and then closed your eyes to the sun.

I've imagined our first kiss so many times, so many different versions of it. Today, I imagine that we'd have spent a perfect day together, swimming on the beach and eating something marvelous out of our hands, like churros, or cups of perfectly ripe fresh fruit, or something flaky and buttery from the pastry shop. And we'd have felt it all day, this light, playful sensation skimming along just under the surface of our conversation, and then it would finally be time for me to go home, but we'd both be stalling saying goodbye, and then something between us would soften and slow down like syrup, and the air would still, and you'd look at me and I'd look at you and we'd just be there, grinning at each other, with a knowing look in our eyes. And we'd each check with the other, without words, using only our eyes, to make sure it was a *yes* for each of us. And then you'd reach the most gentle of hands to my face and softly pinch my chin in your thumb, and run your thumb over my lips, and I'd lean closer. And you'd lean closer, the light between us thinning. And we'd brush our lips together, and time would stop while my chest crystalized into something new. And I'd sip the essence of you, your mouth, your heart, your soul, your kindness, and your warmth. And when we'd pull apart, you'd be glowing and I'd feel like I was glowing too, and I'd murmur, "That was nice," and you'd agree, and then I'd start to get ready to leave and you'd ask, "So, what now?" And we'd pause a moment just looking at each other, and I'd say, "How about you let me know when you're thinking of me." And we'd leave it like that.

But all that was only imagined. We've been friends for years and we've never kissed.

Last time I saw you, I was a little drunk and you were dancing with your arms up like beautiful branches, your eyes bright and glassy. You might have been a little bit high. I snuggled up against you for a song and then snuck away. I wasn't ready to show you the love I feel for you in my heart, in my blood, the way I cherish every single thing about you, all the way into my fingerprints.

Lust Off the Charts

MY LUST IS off the charts. Everything you do is getting me so hot right now. I watched you eat pickles out of a jar and I got instantly wet. You weren't even trying to seduce me. You were just showing me the pickles you made because you know I love that shit. But I thought of the brine and the way your cum smells on my fingers, salty like that, and I saw you open the lid and your face peer over the rim, and I watched you inhale the scent, and then you reached your fingers into the jar and pulled one out and popped it into your mouth and I went crazy. I started salivating. My breathing skipped a beat and got heavy. An alarm went off in my body, revving all the engines. *I want you I want you I want you,* it wailed.

You sent me a picture of dolphins swimming in the harbor, because now with the virus, there are fewer boats and people, and the dolphins are showing up in harbors and stuff, supposedly. Is it real or photoshopped? We don't know. Who cares? It was such a sweet little innocent video, but I perverted it in an instant. The arcs of their backs as they rose up over the slick, shiny water and crested back down again, a whole pod of them, rising and falling like that, made me flush, my eyes bulging, because it was just how my tongue laps over your clit and the waves of your pussy lips, those same quick motions, exactly like that—over and over, that wet sensual flicking and licking.

But, also, it's just you. It's us and the chemistry between us, potent, nearly noxious, intoxicating. Look at what it's doing to me.
Are we dangerous to others in this highly pheromonic state? Only if

we are so fixated on fucking each other that we forget to do things like use our turn signals and stop at traffic lights. Mmm, turn signals. That reminds me of your ears and how much I love to kiss and lick and bite them, and how wild it drives you, how you wiggle and whimper and your fingers reach out, grasping for my wrists. When I do that, it's like I'm steering you by your ears. I can control the entire vehicle of your body. Vehicle. That's a sexy word. I like how it spills through my mouth when I annunciate it: *v e h i c l e.* Would I fuck you in a vehicle, say, at a traffic light? Yes, I would, ravenous and speedy. As long as I didn't get yelled and honked at. That's where I draw the line. I don't like people hating on me when I'm trying to love on someone. And that someone is you. Always you.

If I could reinvent society, I'd create a utopia where everyone had enough and everyone was taken care of and people's hearts would be so nourished and safe that they'd just stay open, you'd be able to see it in their eyes. Everyone would look at each other with sweet melty expressions all the time and that would make them really horny, but not in like an aggressive way, more like in a come-hither way, and the world would live in peace. Rollicking, orgiastic peace.

We'd fuck all our neighbors, with consent, of course: all the lonesome people who miss love and the people who are worried they are getting old and flabby and the people who feel hopeless and detached. We'd breathe hope and vitality back into them, our mouths a bellows to their genitals, and we'd make the world a better place. We'd be this team of soft hands, sweet lips, reassuring words, and sexy prowess, and we could fuck them together or separately, each on a case-by-case basis. Socialism-cum-sexualism has got me all ready to go. Cum. Latin for I'm coming, I'm coming undone, come to me, and come in my mouth.

Speaking of mouths, I was drinking from my travel coffee mug this morning and I started fixating on the little mouth in the lid, how it's the exact shape of your lips when you come, a little parted and turned down at the corners, and then it was like I could hear the sound of your orgasm in the air around me, as if a hundred sexy cherubs were humping the clouds ohh, ohhh, ohhhhh. My pussy exploded in my pants while I was walking home from the coffee shop and I almost tripped into the street.

I couldn't stop looking at the shape of the hole, and then that got me thinking about your other holes. The little starburst of your asshole that I love to run my tongue around. How much I love to hold your gorgeous round ass in my hands, spread your cheeks, and lick you in circles, to kiss that little rosebud like I do your mouth. I love the way it makes you squirm with pleasure and how I can run my hand to your front and rub your clit at the same time. And once I get you all worked up like that, I slide my finger in your cunt while I'm rimming you, and you get all the sensations of my body in two of your holes at once.

I lust for every one of your holes, one at a time, two at a time, let's see, could I get three at a time? Yes, I could. I could finger your cunt and your ass with one hand and kiss your gorgeous mouth all at once. You love it when my hand is spread against your perineum and I have my fingers up your cunt and my thumb up your ass. All it takes is a little shaking of the hand while I fuck you, and my thumb begins to jiggle, and I can feel the way your pussy clenches me. That feels so fucking good. When I taste your fermented sex sweat on my lips, I lose my shit.

Let's see, how else could I fuck you in three holes at once? I could fuck you with a strap-on from behind, rub your clit, and tongue your ear. Your ear counts as a hole. But it's hard to resist your mouth. Could I kiss your mouth, fuck your juicy cunt with one hand, and use my other hand to fuck your asshole? I'd have to exercise my wrists a bit. Maybe laying down would be too hard, but I could do that standing up. Let's try it next time you come over. We could do it in the shower, maybe, or in the kitchen. I'd love to bend you over my kitchen counter and explore every ripe fruit in the tree of your body. I want to eat you alive, sweetheart.

It's all I've ever wanted. Everything you do and say, every way you move, and every time I even think of you, you make me wet, you get me hot, you make me come.

We were eating lunch and you put a spoonful of curry into your mouth, and I said *ahhhh* really loudly, and my mouth dropped and my whole body slumped into my seat. It was so embarrassing. We were in a restaurant! I just can't contain myself around you. I saw that shiny steel spoon slip into your open mouth and all I could think about was replacing that spoon with my tongue. How much I want to have you on the couch, feeling you up and pressed against you and sliding my tongue into the honeydew hollow of your mouth.

Goddamn. I want to run my tongue over the ridges of your mouth. I want to suck your tongue and bite your lips. I want to explore the entirety of your lips, your teeth, your palate, your spit. I want your taste overpowering the taste of my own mouth. I want to inhale your essence, breathe you into me, and slurp up your sweetness.

I want you in the shower, your hand against the wall, arm bracing your weight, my cock inside your heavenly cunt, a butt plug snug in your asshole, and the thump, thump, thump of my hips as they crash against the shore of your ass, water splashing everywhere. I want to feel the chasm and spasm of your orgasm with my eyes shut and my wet hair slapping in my face. I want to grab ahold of your hair and steer you into the surf of your next climax. We will ride it together, and you will take it deep for me, so deep I lose my edges, so deep I fall into the abyss of my lust.

And in the dark of the abyss I see the next shiny thing that sets me off. It's just a glimmer now. Let me come closer. I'm groping. I can't see it yet. Oh, *groping*. Groping is hot. Know what I want to grope? You. Your tits. I want your tits in my hands. You laugh and press your hips to mine. Oh shit. Here I go again.

Tied Up And Waiting

IT WAS HER idea to tie me to the chair. She wrapped a pair of stockings around my wrists and knotted them tight. A knee sock around each of my ankles. A silk scarf blindfolded my eyes. She had already taken off all my clothes. I felt her fingers running over my chest, my jaw, my shoulders. And then she left. My cock was getting stiff, and when I thought of her, of what she might look like right now, it did that twitch thing.

Some sultry twinkly music started playing from the stereo. I'd heard her play this before but never paid much attention to it. Now it sounded velvety and alluring. I could sense the warmth of candlelight. I felt her legs brush up against me and then her breath was on my skin. My belly. One nipple. Holy shit. And then the other.

We'd never done anything like this before. Oh, I guess when we were first dating we made out with more passion, but even then it was just like, I don't know, regular? I'd put my arm around her, lean in, we'd start kissing, you know. We made out, had sex, it was good. I mean, I don't think we would have gotten married if it wasn't good, right? It's always been good, at least for me, and I think for her, but in the last ten years, with the kids and work and juggling our parents' ailing health in turn, it's like our chemistry's fallen slack.

That's why tonight is such a surprise.

She's right there beyond the blindfold. I can just see a little bit of thigh and lace peeking under the edge. Her confidence is so hot. I've never seen her like this before. What's gotten into her? Is it that new book group she joined?

I don't know what's different, I'm just so fucking excited. She's straddling my legs now, standing over me. Oh gawd, I can feel her underwear grazing my thigh and it's wet. "Hey baby," I say. "Lemme touch you."

"*Shhhh,*" she whispers in my ear, "It's my turn now."

I can feel her breasts almost touching my face, the silk on her bra, just barely grazing me. Now she's sitting on me, and I can feel her pussy resting lightly on my cock. She's pressing her chest to my chest and licking my ear. Holy shit, I have such a huge hard-on. Oh, I want to be inside her so badly, but I don't want her to stop this seduction.

"I want you so badly," I whisper into her ear.

"You'll have to wait," she teases. "Until *I'm* ready for *you.*"

What would I do if she untied me right now? I'd want to leap on her and thrust my cock inside her and just start pumping away. But I don't think that's what she wants. I'd have to restrain myself. I'd have to hold back, and touch her, feel her body all over, appreciate her skin, her lusciousness, her fullness. I'd kiss her pussy and rub my tongue all over her thighs and belly. I'd suck on her lips and try not to think about my cock. I could do it. I could wait.

And then maybe I could even make her wait. She'd get so revved up, and I can just imagine her grinding her hips in the air, and I'd grip her thighs and not let my cock inside her just yet, just barely let the tip touch her, just softly, and then I'd wait until she moaned, and give her a little more, just a touch of the head, hardly anything, and I'd wait until she asked again, and then just a little more, for a second, and then I'd withdraw and watch her and kiss her and touch her, and I think I could even wait until she begged me for it, and then, and only then, enter her so slowly, and so thoughtfully, my cock screwing gently into her, no thrusting, no pumping, not this time. That's what I want. I want to know how she likes that.

My cock is pointing up in the air like the mast on a ship. I'm not used to being trapped in a chair like this. I'm used to having a hand, mine or hers, or a thigh or a mouth there, some sheets entangling us, and lots of touching. This feels so, I don't know, exposed. She's behind me know, rubbing her tits against the back of my neck and running her fingers around my nipples in little circles. That feels amazing. My lord, I've never been touched like that before. It's making my cock go crazy, like there's a geyser inside it bursting with heat.

"Oh, honey," I moan. "Let me just touch you. Let me grab your ass. Please," I beg.

She unties one wrist but presses my arm to the chair arm while she stuffs her nipple in my mouth. I can hardly breathe. I want to devour her. She unties the other wrist and smacks my hands on her ass, and I have this urge to grab her so hard I'd hurt her. I hold back. But to my surprise, I'm just moaning with her tittie in my mouth and my hands trying to hold her without grasping her too tight, and I start to cry. I actually start to make whimpering sounds and tears are rolling down my cheeks.

"You okay, baby?" she asks.

"Yes, yes," I mutter as the tears roll down.

I press her ass toward my face 'til I'm kissing her all over her belly, licking the line of her C-section scar, licking the creases of her thighs. I can smell her, juicy and dripping, and I just can't hold back any longer. I push my mouth into her pussy like I'm sucking the pit from a fruit. She gasps and starts to arch and moan. I've never hungered for anything like this in my life. I'm just kissing and sucking and tasting and loving her. I can't get enough. She comes, hard, screaming, pulling my hair, and a wash of warm sweet fluid crashes into my lap. I use my hands to thrust inside her while my cock's there waiting, dying, to be next.

"You want this, babe?" I ask over and over again.

"Yes," she says, "yes yes yes."

She's coming in spasms and gushes, and I'm asking her what she wants. She clasps her hand over my mouth and sinks onto my cock with her slick, hot pussy. I can hardly handle the sensation. It's everything everywhere all at once. I'm electrified.

I grab her hips and suck her chest, and she's rocking her hips in hula hoops against my cock, and it's rubbing this warm gooey sensation from my asshole through my balls up into my heart and through the tip of my cock. I've never, never, been fucked like this before. I'm crying out her name, and again the tears are flowing, and I'm so full of gratitude and love for my wife. I start to come, I can feel it, but nothing gushes out. It's like a long, slow build, like that feeling of being at the top of a hill and then you're sledding down and down and down, and it lasts so long, there's no end.

At The Old Hitch Saloon

LESLIE WAS AN old-school butch, and I knew as soon as I walked in the room that I wanted to bang her. Jeans tight around her thighs. Polished up Doc Martens. Buddy Holly glasses. Pompadour. She was wearing a vest and an ascot. A real dandy. Just my type. I took my jacket off, leaned over the pool table for my next shot, and narrowed my eyes on her frame. I watched her have a drink with her pals—a mix of older, hip queers and a group of women who looked like a softball team, with big muscles, cottony bangs, scraggly mullets, and hands like paws.

I went back to Brie, who was mid-shot aiming a blue stripe into the corner pocket, and high-fived her when she made it. We've always cheered each other on, even when we're technically competing. "Check out the dandy with the yellow ascot," I whispered, nudging her in the Dandy's direction.

"Oh, you go girl," Brie said, a little too loudly. "I might just take the rest of the team." Brie spun around slowly and arched her back like a bow against her pool cue. One of the softball players looked up quick, square jaw crinkling with a slow grin, and Brie returned it.

Fuck, I thought, *Brie gets all the hotties.* She's a textbook babe. Tan, curvy, eyelashes as thick as fur, pouty lips. She's not my type, but as her best friend, I happen to know she has a gorgeous bush. Even though you can't see it through her pants or anything, it's like you can sense it. Your gaydar picks up on it, all beep, beep, beep. It's dark and thick and soft, like big hair in the 80s, a perfect triangle, huge. I don't give a fuck what's popular in porn these days, whatever kind of skimpy strips and stubbly bald puss they say is the style, the queer lovers I've known like a bush, a real deal bush I tell you. My best friend Brie is a top-notch bush in cute wrapping paper. And she knew it. You could practically taste the cum smell wafting off her.

If lezzes and masculine-of-center enbies like these were teenage boys—oh and you know that sometimes you mistake them, when you're all *heyyy* to what you think is a forty-five-year-old tomboy or hot queer person with a fade strutting down the sidewalk, and then it's a dude, and not just a dude, but, like, a fifteen-year-old gawky high school student; the worst kind of mistake, some folks just don't know what we have to put up with—anyway, if the softball players here were actually teenage boys, Brie would be the kind of babe they'd buy a poster of to hang in their rooms. Brie, with a cherry dangling between her poofy lips, in cut-off jeans and a see-through crop top. Some shit like that. The whole team would have her picture up, trust me. I could imagine them each making out with the poster: tracing her lips and all *hey baby,* or humping it against the wall, or jerking off in their beds with it tacked to the slanted ceiling.

"You done with that cue?" A hand against my elbow, soft, firm. A button-up plaid cuff. Oh shit, the Dandy! I was twirling the pool cue between my legs, lost in my reverie. Oh my god, how embarrassing. I stammered to explain that we were probably done, I just needed to check in with my friend, that we'd kind of lost track of the game. And the Dandy said, "Oh no, I was enjoying watching you play. I was gonna ask if you wanted to play me." The Dandy gave me puppy eyes. *Play?*

I eyed the Dandy and smiled back. Oh, I'd play. We racked them up. Brie handed her cue over to the Dandy, who said, "Hi, I'm Leslie, pronouns they/them." Oops, I'd been assuming "she/her" pronouns in my mind. Noted. Good thing they told me. I introduced myself, named my pronouns, and racked up the balls. Leslie invited me to break, and we both laughed when I accidentally banked one of each.

"So, which do you want?" they asked, "solids or stripes?"

"Do I get to pick?" I asked.

"Oh, you always get to pick," the Dandy said coyly.

"Is that what you tell all the ladies?" I asked.

"Maybe something like that," they said, and they tipped their chin at me in that classic masc-of-center way.

"Okay," I said. "Well, in that case . . . I pick you." I was feeling bold and the night held the promise of adventure. Leslie blushed and tugged at their ascot and looked down at the floor. I stepped closer and whispered in their ear, "I want to take you home with me tonight."

I pulled back to look them in the eye, to give them some glimmer, show them I was serious. And curious. And hungry. I wanted them to feel it. They took a deep breath and sized me up, mostly my face, getting a read on me and my vibe. They smiled with a little nod, put their elbow out to the side, and said, "Get your bag and go tell your friend goodbye."

After a quick explanation and a good luck kiss from Brie, who had scooted into the booth to sling back some beers with the softball team, I took Leslie's arm and was escorted from the bar towards a Subaru.

"Hey," I said, grabbing onto their wrist. I made a turn around to the brick wall, pressed my body up against theirs, breathing in the scent of neck and hair, looking up at Leslie, just waiting for a first kiss. I felt flirty as hell, a mix of aggressive and reserved, but I like my lover to make the first move. The chorus of "Everywhere" was tinkling from inside the bar when Leslie leaned in to kiss me. Soft at first, a graze of lips, fingers finding my hair, my hips.

Stumbling into the dark apartment, I dragged the Dandy around with me, my fingers in their belt loops, while I locked the door and pulled the curtains, put on my make-out playlist, and lit a candle. Then we kissed and groped and pressed into each other, clothes on, getting the feel of each other's bodies and lips.

"What do you like?" I whispered into their ear in the dark. "Maybe you'll tell me some, and maybe you'll show me some, and maybe I'll figure some out myself, hmm?"

Leslie kept kissing me and bit my lip, hitting on something I really like. I responded by grabbing the flesh of their waist and digging my fingernails in. They inhaled quick and sharp, and I did it again, this time longer. I put their hand on my fly and pressed their fingers to un-button it.

They ran their fingers against the top of my panties and said, "I'd like for you to drop your pants." Still kissing, I stuck my ass out and started to peel my pants down. I took Leslie's hand and pressed it to my naked belly, and then unlocked our lips so they could watch me perform, churning my hips and stripping off my clothes slowly, my eyes focused on that sexy butch face. "Fuck," the Dandy breathed.

"Will you?" I asked, placing their hand on my bush.

"This?" Leslie asked, slipping a finger in.

"Yes," I moaned.

"You like this?" Hot whisper, finger slipping in and out of my slick pussy.

"Oh yes," I sighed.

"More?"

"Uh huh."

Leslie fucked me thicker, three fingers then four, backing me up against the wall. I was lifted up and pressed, their crotch to mine, one arm cupping my ass, the other hand still going in and out, tongue on my tits, teeth trapping my nipple in a tight little bite. My hips rocking hard against theirs, I kept moaning and circling my neck, squeezing my toes. I liked that: pinned to the wall, suspended, a strong arm under my ass, fingers pumping inside me.

I gasped, "You like this?" trying to get the words out, wanting to hear the answer.

"Yes," came the answer, in a serious voice, "I really like fucking you."

"Take me to the bed," I ordered, interrupting us mid-fuck.

"Not yet," they teased, and they kept going. Oh, I loved that. *Make me wait,* I thought. I wanted to turn the tables so I could find out what else they liked, but they weren't letting me. I stretched my neck toward their ear and licked it, taking pleasure when they shuddered. I licked all around their ear and bit their earlobe, satisfied that their hips were moving harder. I think their knees were getting weak because they did let me down then, and we stumbled onto the bed, wet with sweat and pussy and spit.

"May I?" I asked, my hand on their fly.

"Nope," was the quick reply, and a palm put over mine.

"Okay," I said, "Let's see what else you like." I wiggled down their body, softly blowing against their neck, their arm, licking their fingers, and breathing hot air over their crotch through their jeans. The Dandy exhaled deeply. "Yes?" I asked.

"Yeah," was the answer. So I did it again and ground my chin against their pubic bone, feeling the wet and heat, guessing where their clit was, and lightening my touch, rubbing my nose and cheek around and around, inhaling a lush scent through the denim, getting this Dandy going. I moved up to their neck, licking and nipping, and slipped my knee between their legs, giving them my thigh to grind against. Oh, yes, I could feel Leslie liked that.

I watched their muscles tighten at first and then melt, mouth drooping, pussy still grinding my thigh, slower now. "You like getting fucked lying down or standing up, hot stuff?" I asked. Leslie just looked at me with puppy eyes.

I put my hands on their shoulders and pressed my weight down. "Do you like being fucked by me like this?" I asked.

"Yes," I heard.

"Do you feel me fucking you right now?" I asked, exaggerating the thrust of my hips, flint-striking our imaginations. "You want to be my little dandy?" I asked, wondering if they'd like flipping around. They nodded with squinted pleasure eyes. "Let me grind against your ass?" I asked.

"Yes," they hissed.

"Roll over," I instructed, guiding their body so they lay on their belly. I ran my hands around in circles over their ass, then up and down their rib cage and neck, through their hair real quick. I trailed my hand down their spine, and then gripped their hips tight and lifted up their voluminous ass. I pressed my pubic bone against them, hard through the denim. I imagined a long pulsing cock, swollen at the tip, slipping down Leslie's crack. I could almost feel it. So could Leslie, I could tell by the gasp and clenched glutes.

I moved one hand around and snaked it under their waistband. "This okay?" I murmured.

"Mmm," they moaned, "yes, please." I thrust the idea of a cock between Leslie's ass cheeks, and held it there like you would, until they got used to it, listening to their breath catch, feeling this lust take over me and lurch into my hips. And then I just gripped their hips and started thrusting strong and hot into their ass, like I had a real dick or a silicone cock, except there wasn't one, it was just our imaginations, and I got so into it, I really felt like I was deep inside, gripped by their ass in a pleasure hold, and I started to feel this build in me, like I was about to come. And Leslie was writhing, and I kept grabbing their flesh, their back, their waist, their ass, and fucking them faster and wilder, and my clit was getting so hot and huge, and I just couldn't stop, I came like a fucking avalanche. And so did Leslie. Guess I turned out to be quite the dandy myself.

What's Your Heaven?

"**WHEN YOU GET** to Heaven, there's a long line of girls bent over wagging their fannies at you and waiting to be screwed."

That's what my friend Giles told me when we were lying under the swaying trees after baseball practice.

"That is *if* you like girls," he explained.

I imagined a long line of chorus legs in red high heels with seams painted up the backs of their legs that disappeared just under their asses. With their hands on their knees, they look over their shoulders all sexy, with big red movie star lips and thick black eyelashes.

"Fucking angels," he said knowingly. "That's what they are, *fucking* angels. And when it's your turn, they are there all lined up waiting for you. You get to be surrounded by clouds and fuck as many pussies as you want. And you can try all of them or you can pick the fanny you like best and just hammer away, and that girl will be the happiest angel in cloudland."

I opened my eyes to the blue and the clouds and imagined them up there waiting for me. My prick was getting stiff in my shorts.

"If you're gay," Giles said, "all the gay angels line up, with their lavender wings folded behind them, and the tufts of their feathers form a crown on their heads making them look really innocent. They stand side by side, like a row of soldiers, and you can go up and down the row giving them hand jobs and asking them to blow you. Then, at your command, they bend over, and you can have any or all their asses. You can fuck them 'til your dick falls off. Which it won't, because this is Heaven."

We were lying under the ponderosa pines by a little stream when

he told me this. There was no one around. You could hear water bur-
bling and the birds trilling and the wind rustling the tree limbs. There
were slants of light all around, and the dust in the air was sparkling.
The sky was suddenly pulsing, the blue more vibrant than before. The
clouds parting now had a new meaning, as I imagined the orgy under-
way way above me.

In my mind then, it was an orgy, but when I think back on it now,
it's not so much an orgy as it is fuck gluttony.

"Which would *you* want," Giles asked, "the gay version or the
girls?"

My mind started buzzing. I didn't know what to say. Both stories
tickled me in the taint and got me sweating. I knew I was supposed to
say I wanted the girls, but Giles was making it so easy to want the guys.
He made it sound so natural. What if *he* wanted the guys too?

I looked up at the sky for an answer. The clouds were dripping
with cum.

"I don't know," I stammered, "What, what would—what about
you?"

Giles sighed and let his legs flop open on the blanket. I could see
his boner through his pants. He let his hand graze it and plucked at his
underwear. "Honestly," he said, "I think I'd take the guys."

I swallowed, hard. Here was a guy in the woods with a hard-on
telling me he liked other guys and not only that, but that he thought
about sex with them. *This might be it,* I told myself. This really might
be it.

Giles went on, filling the silence between us. "I mean, it's a tough
call," he said. "I like knockers. I'd like to get my hands on every pair.
But when I think of all those men with tight asses all lined up, I just go
a bit mad." Giles looked at me out the side of his eye. "You know?" he
asked, with a smile.

I couldn't find the words. It's like my brain vaporized and I forgot
language. I don't know how much time passed. And then I managed
to ask him, "What would you do? Fuck them or go for the blow jobs?"

Giles rolled over on his side to face me. "Do you want me to show you?"

I nodded.

He curled his finger into the waistband of my pants and snapped it. "Are you my angel then?" he asked, coyly.

"Yeah," I said, "Okay. I'll be your, uh, angel. Yes."

Yes.

Bifurious (Part Two)

WHEN I WALKED into their open floor mid-century rental, I smelled of the husband's exquisite armpits, and I still felt the aftershocks of his thrusting penis between my legs. My thighs were sticky. The wife leapt up to greet me and offered to bathe me. She took me by the hand to the bathroom and closed the door. She chucked the stopper in the drain, turned the water on hot, and spun around to meet me. She twisted her hair up in a quick bun, stabbed it with a pencil, and started to unbutton her blouse, all while giving me a very clear I-want-you look. Steam began to build in the tiny room, and sweat bubbled the mirrors and glass. Then she flung the door open.

"While I bathe you, I want you to watch the men," she announced.

Through the bathroom door I had a clear view into the living room, where the men were clinking tumblers of bourbon and shifting logs in the fireplace with wrought iron pokers. I could see them passing a joint back and forth. The husband started giggling, and the boyfriend went into the kitchen to rummage around in the fridge. He came back with an artisanal sausage, the kind that tastes like buttered smoke and is locally made with shit like fennel pollen and some kind of fermented sap. He tore the paper off and gnashed a hunk, and they passed it back and forth while talking excitedly about all the pussy they'd been getting from us of late. And one of them said, yes, they were both blessed with the best two pussies on the planet, *and*—what he really had been jonesing for today was a hot, hard cock.

In the bathroom, the wife was down to her bra and stockings. She was wearing one of those sexy garters with all the straps. I was impressed. Did she always dress like this? I made a mental note to up my wardrobe a notch. Having never worn one, I didn't quite understand how to work the contraption, so I was hoping she wouldn't expect me to seductively remove it or anything. She took a step closer.

"Come here," she whispered, "Let me take these off." She slipped my blouse and pants off and grinned when she saw I wasn't wearing any panties. They were stuffed in her husband's jacket pocket.

"Was my husband's cock in here?" she asked, tickling my mons with her index finger. I nodded. To my surprise, she wriggled her panties off without removing the garter. Now I had access to her sexpot pussy and also the thrill of her elegant lingerie. The faucet was gushing hot bubbling water.

Through the doorway, I watched the boyfriend lick the sausage suggestively and mock giving it a little blow job, as if to ask, *want to?* He performed this to the husband, but I knew he was doing it for our entertainment. He wiggled his eyebrows and laughed. The husband took the sausage and clasped his lips around the meat, running the O of his mouth up and down, deep throating the meat. Well, that made it pretty clear.

I have such a thing for gay porn, and the wife knew it. Here she was orchestrating this whole scenario. She'd probably asked her boyfriend to seduce her husband in front of me. She knew the husband wanted the boyfriend and that I wanted to see the men together and that she wanted me. What a little maestro the wife was turning out to be!

She abruptly turned the water off and tossed some oil and salt and flower petals into the tub, leaning over the bath in her striking bra and garter, stirring the water with her toes. When she rose, she held out her hand like a gentleman inviting a lady to step over a puddle, and escorted me into the steamy tub. I stood there in the water, keeping my eyes on the men in the next room, and she began to sponge me over with fragrant suds. "Does that feel nice?" she purred, pressing my shoulder so that I sat down and sank into the tub.

"Yes," I said, closing my eyes and tipping my head back.

I imagined what the men were up to and turned up the attention in my ears. The fire was popping and crackling while two flies were unzipping. Tuning in to the subtlest sounds, I thought I could hear a flannel and a Henley going overhead and then falling to the floor. Jeans were being peeled off. I could hear the unzip sound and the clink of a belt buckle on the floor. Surely socks were being removed too. And skivvies. I opened my eyes to see two men buck naked, their silhouettes against the orange flames. I felt caught between watching the action and closing my eyes to listen, letting the scene play out in my mind's eye. It was impossible to do both. I'd just close my eyes for one more moment.

I felt the wife's legs step into the tub, sidle up, and squeeze my sides. I opened my eyes to see a hairy mound of pussy with slick brownish ruffles hovering above me, framed by her divine thighs, with the garter straps all around like the gussets of the Eiffel Tower. She squatted slowly, bringing her dangling pussy lips closer to my face. I inhaled her sweat as her quivering, bearded sex lowered slowly, like a piano being moved out the window of a high rise to the ground floor. I clasped her hips to guide her down. She gripped the sides of the tub, and her luscious tits came closer. A little pearly droplet on her bush gleamed like morning dew. I opened my mouth wide.

While I was mouthing the wife with thick licks of my tongue, I watched the scene of the men in my mind. One man's lips encircled another man's prick, with repetitive sliding and thrusting. Arched backs and stiff abs. His hands pressing down on his head. His hands clasped about his calves. I could hear grunts and gasps and groans.

Sucking the wife's pussy was a mouthful. Her lips were glossy and meaty. Her bush kept tickling the insides of my nostrils. I sucked and chewed lightly on her pussy lips while she oohed and ahhed. When I poked my tongue into her pleasure hole, she yelped and settled more heavily onto my face. Her cum was creamy and delightfully pungent.

The garter ribbons on her thighs were super hot. The bath was so lush and aromatic. The men were getting it on in the next room. The whole scene was turning me on to the extreme.

From that moment on, I couldn't stop. I arched my tongue and slid it in and out of her, faster and faster and deeper and deeper, as I grabbed her ass and mashed her into my mouth. By this point, she was heaving and clenching the sides of the tub, her cunt held captive by my mouth. She started chanting *omigawd omigawd*. When she came, she was softly screaming, breathy like a dry reed. She didn't want to wake the kids. Her pussy earthquaked against my chin.

She slid like liquid into the water and settled at the opposite end of the tub, our legs end to end, her feet in my crotch. "Go on and look," she said, and I turned my head to witness the hot fuck taking place in the living room. That was my man taking some thick cock. His hands were on the mantle and his ass was being pounded by the boyfriend. His legs were shaking, and a string of spit was hanging down his chin. That's how hard he was getting fucked. He couldn't even close his mouth. Drool pooled on the hearth.

The boyfriend was holding the husband's skinny hips like the wheel of a car and slamming over and over again into the puckered hole gaping for more. The husband had told me how much he loved being fucked like this. I'd fucked him similarly with a dildo, but I hadn't been as rough as the boyfriend was being now. I know he'd been craving that sensation, getting filled up so big like that, getting that much stimulus and intensity. I could tell it drove him into a lust-filled frenzy. That cock inside him was fresh from his wife's lascivious cunt. His cock, which it appeared the boyfriend was gripping, had been marinating in my pussy only an hour before while he thrust the orgasm out of me in the pool room.

I licked my lips and smiled at the wife. She was flopped at the other end of the tub, her legs entwined with mine, her arms lank over the rim, her head lolled back with sleepy satisfaction. People look so extra beautiful when they are freshly fucked.

She opened her eyes when she heard her boyfriend and husband start to come at the same time. One of them sounded like a balloon letting out air, and the other like an alto tea kettle. These people. They need to invest in soundproof walls if we are going to keep this up. But the wife didn't seem worried. She looked like a Cheshire cat.

I gasped when I sensed the boyfriend's cum shoot into the husband, and felt a spasm rock my pussy when I saw the husband's cum splat onto the fire screen. I closed my eyes to their panting and heavy breathing, and thought about how lucky I was to have landed in this foursome. I wasn't even looking for it. It just fell in my lap. No pun intended. Next, I wanted to try on the boyfriend. I'd had my eye on that thick cock of his. I like them wide and ropy like that. I figured we could get into some fun trouble together.

Cachonda Fever

bb you have privacy?

yesssssss

waz up

i want you
N
O
W
me pones cachonda

siiiiiiii

nena

what do u want to do to me?

I want to clamp yr nipples

mmmm

handcuff you
and blindfold yr eyes

yyyy?

graze your whole body
with my
nipples and bush

oooh cariño

te quiero
chest to chest
coño a coño
in my arms

i'm ready and dripping

bb
and your cock?
¿él está aquí?

and my cock is here too

¿quién?
¿el dorado?

siiii
the tip of my cock
in yr mouth

i love to blow u bb

oh bb
my cock loves when u blow me
pero
ur other mouth

ahhh mmm

mi coño favorito

[peach] [water squirt]

[flames] [drool face]
wet hard hot cock
c o m i n g
btw your thighs

siiii pf

up yr crack

mmm

just teasing
no cock for you

no cock for me??
[sad anguish face]

not yet
you have to work for it

what do i have to do
[prayer emoticon]

you have to take me first

                                          oh yes i will

                                           ven a mi

I want to sit on your face

                                         rolling over 4 u

                                         gimme yr juices

                                           mmmm

                                         i can taste you

                                I [heart] to suck ur clit

HARDER

                                  don't scream mi amor

                                    you cum so fast

why cant i scream

                                      neighbors!

ok neighbors...

                                          shhh

i'm whispering in your ear I WANT YOU
I WANT YOUR COCK

                                       me encanta

while I bite your ear
and neck

                                      i love that too

and your nipple

                                          oh fuck

ima stay here a minute
got yr nipple btw my tongue + teeth

                                    callllllliente

got my hands tight on your hips
i can smell you
u smell sooo good bb
i got a hard hot cock for you

                                      i want it NOW

i'm gonna fuck you with this cock

                                        give it to me

AHORA

i got u bb

hard
harder

yo te follo

faster

tan duro

u make me cuuuummm

you like my cock bb

me encanta
i want all of u

you drive me wild
te quiero tanto

y yo a ti
mi amante
y tu exquisito chocho

Cinderella Subversion

THIS IS THE story of a pervy prince and a passionate pussy. And in this tale, the prince wasn't a manipulative prick, at least, he didn't mean to be a perv, he was just a total hunk who was a little dumb and who had a spell cast upon his cock. The spell led him like a horse drawn by a carrot throughout the entire village searching for the perfect pussy. And this perfect pussy wasn't about aesthetics or anything like that, it was about a magnetism to ecstasy, a hidden vibe in the cunt and the cock that pulled them together like a lock and key that clicked open the doors of salacious copulation. And, boy, was it needed. A rampant scourge of sexual constipation had consumed the entire kingdom.

So, here's the prince in his chariot, the horses near mad with turning this way and that as the servants and drivers attend to every minuscule whim of the prince's erect cock as it twitches like the needle of a compass, sensing the pheromones of the entire village.

"That way!" the prince decries. "No, *that* way!"

All eyes on his throbbing dick.

Dust shrouds the streets as the chariot lurches through each neighborhood, the cock red and gristly, until the Prince starts to moan, and everyone notices the cock has a little bead of pre-cum pearling at the tip. It's bobbing into a line of drool due to the rollicking ride.

"*STOP!*" the Prince's attendant proclaims.

The Prince licks his lips and leaps off the helm before the chariot has come to a stop, his cock bobbing before him, through the slit in his pants.

"My penis telleth me that this is the palace of the imperial pussy," the Prince decries in his weird, formal, lispy, entitled voice.

He struts up to a cottage with marigolds bedecking the windows.

The door flings open and an old man pushes his wife out the door, her dress swooshing the grass and her eyeglasses akimbo.

"*That is not my pussy!*" the Prince roars.

His helmsmen shove the old man out of the way.

The Prince storms the house.

There, seated at a vanity, a beautiful woman of marriageable age is combing her hair.

"Come in," she purrs to the prince. "I've been expecting you."

The Prince is, for once, speechless.

"My pussy is the one you seek," she announces. "It throbs and glistens beneath my skirt in all manner of divine ecstasy. I know, because I pleasure it daily."

The Prince goes slack-jawed.

"If you," the woman says, eyes firm toward the prince, "can maketh me come with more pleasure than I giveth myself, I will surrender myself to you and the kingdom forevermore."

The Prince's dick is like a beagle hot for a wounded fox. He can barely tame it. It feels as if it might burst forth from his pantaloons and attack her.

"On ONE condition!" the woman announces. "That forever after, when I am Queen, I chooseth my pleasure—how and when I like it—whether it is your cock that giveth or another. I may take a servant or a chambermaid or a woman of the court or a deacon—whomever I want, and you must allow it."

"Anything, anything," the Prince agrees, as his cock elongates another inch or two, something he never thought possible.

The woman lifts her skirt to reveal a pussy swollen to the size of a grapefruit, dripping honey-like juices, perfuming the room with wild ambrosia. All the Prince's helmsmen swoon and pass out. The woman makes her way over the Prince and announces, "I will receive you now."

And in the *happily ever after*, the soil hummed like an earthquake and the sky shook like thunder. The moaning and rollicking and humping and groaning lit up the entire village with a passion and fervor they'd never felt before. They say that all the tulips bloomed within moments with large sighs, and that an entire field of sunflowers turned their large heads to look, and that eggplants ripened in an instant, slick and burnished purple and swollen, and that the tomatoes burst their seems, drooling sunlit spit all over the vine.

Meet Me in the Salish Sea

WE HAD PICKED a place to meet. Because she lived in Victoria and I lived in Seattle. The premise was that I would interview her because I admired her work, and the exhibition she'd just had was among my favorites. But I couldn't make it all the way to Canada for the holiday weekend. I could take a ferry to an island halfway, where she had a cabin. So that's what we planned.

I threw my camping gear in the trunk and hit the road. On the way up I called a friend and told him of my plan to interview the artist, admitting my secret crush. I told him how the artist had read my last novel and emailed me to say how much she loved it. I returned the favor and offered an interview.

He googled a picture and said, "I know her."

"What?" I exclaimed.

Yes, he explained, they'd been at a party together, a queer back-yard barbeque. She came with a friend of ours, another artist, and they'd talked over glasses of whiskey by the fire. She was butch and he is trans and they had a bro moment together, that kind of instant camaraderie, and they each shared their dreams of finding love. "I could see you together," he said. "She's smart and sexy, really hot."

"I know!" I said. "And crazy talented. So, she's single?" I asked, my voice catching in my throat.

"She was last summer," he replied.

I had already snooped around online enough to guess that if there was a woman in her life, it was not made public. She seemed like an introvert, a bit of a loner. Sparkly eyes, thick thighs, just my type.

On the drive up, I couldn't stop thinking about her. My only distractions were glimpses of the bright sudden sea as I swung around curves through the forest. While on the ferry I imagined our seduction, the flirting, the tender lean in, the inevitable thrashing. I wanted her to dominate me. At the beginning, we'd both be sensing each other to gauge interest. Would she be comfortable merging the professional with the personal? Was it ludicrous that I was even entertaining this notion? I'd have to be careful so that I didn't make a fool of myself and ruin a career opportunity.

"Keep the interview professional," I said aloud, under my breath, trying to make a pact with myself. *And then after you can flirt, but just slightly, and only if she returns your glances with interest.* This seemed like a sound plan, but then I'd interrupt myself with an image of her fucking me against a tree in the woods. *Focus!* I slapped the inside of my mind.

But then I saw her leaning in to kiss me for the first time, real slow, her eyes bright and sharp. *I really want her*, I admitted. Huge crush, borderline obsession. And I'm only saying borderline to not sound like a creep. *I'm excited*, I reasoned. Please let her feel it too. Please let her want me. Please let her feel my desire. Even from afar.

"I want you," I whispered aloud, like an incantation cast into the sea breeze rumbling over the tapestry of the water and the ruffled wake of the ferry. Any butch worth her salt, I hoped and prayed, would hear my siren's call.

We had agreed to meet at the cabin. I brought my recorder as planned, along with a cooler of artisanal beer, mineral water, apples, and nuts. In case things went the way I wanted, I had a bottle of cognac stashed in my glove box. I had no idea what she might want, but I wanted to be prepared for anything.

I sat in the car a moment, wondering if she would come out to greet me or if I should knock on the door. Or wait on the porch? She hadn't said. Do I bring the cooler or leave it for now? I was overthinking this. *Take a deep breath*, I self-instructed. My nerves felt like they were gripping my blood vessels like reigns.

From the car, I glanced at the cabin. I saw a head bob through the window, and it looked like she was wearing a towel. Oh my lord. Was she naked under it? Had she forgotten I was coming and just gotten out of the shower? Or, did she take a shower *because* I was coming? My heart was throbbing in my chest and I could feel my pussy drooling into my pants.

Would the crush be requited?

Would we have the chemistry I longed for?

"Carpe diem," I muttered as I got out of the car, stumbled down the walkway, and knocked on the heavy wooden door. She answered the door while scruffing the towel against her head. Sparkling eyes. Gleaming straight teeth. She was wearing a wet swimsuit, the sports bra type with shorts.

We shook hands.

"I couldn't resist a quick dip," she said with a big smile. "I thought about waiting for you but didn't know if you'd have brought a suit."

I just stared. And then I opened my mouth and closed it twice like a fish.

She brought me in and threw together a snack for us, thick slabs of bread with cheese and homemade jam and hunks of cucumbers cranked over with sea salt. While she lumbered about the kitchen, I checked out her digs. Hand-turned wooden bowls, smooth-edged ceramics, woven rugs, signed and framed Joan Armatrading album. No evidence of a current girlfriend.

We settled down on the deck and I cracked open two beers, turned the recorder on, and started asking her questions. We had an interesting, easy, and candid professional conversation with plenty of material for a strong article.

The interview was winding down, but the recorder was still on.

"So, do you have any regrets in life?" I asked. She was lying in the sun, her suit dry now, the sun glowing on her skin.

"Professionally?" she asked.

"Oh, sure," I stammered. "Or personally, either way. Or both."

She laughed, her teeth bright in the sun.

"Nope, not my style," she said. "Although if I could rewind time, I would've handled a few personal things differently, but I didn't know how then."

"Care to elaborate?" I asked impulsively, before I realized that talking about exes was not a good segue toward making a move.

"You wanna go there?" She laughed and stood up. "I have a better idea. Do you like to swim?"

"Yes."

"Did you bring a suit?"

Well, I did not bring a suit. I'd not thought to.

"Not exactly," I said, "but I could manage." I was wearing a decent enough bra and underwear combo to pass.

"Great," she said. "See that willow tree over there?" She pointed to a green form across the water. "It's one of my favorite spots."

"Okay," I said.

It looked like a fairly easy swim, a little long for me maybe, but I'd be fine.

"And then you can't bring *that* with you!" she chortled, pointing to my recorder.

"Alright," I said.

She dove in.

I followed.

Once on the island, she shook off like a wet dog and flopped down in the grass on an old patchwork quilt I guess she just left there fading in the sun. I wasn't too far behind, doing my best breaststroke dog-paddle combo. The water was cool and silky against my limbs. What a surprise this day was turning out to be. Swimming? Heading for an *island* alone with the artist? It all seemed so unreal.

I climbed out of the water trying to look cool and collected. *No big deal,* I professed silently, *I swim in my underwear to random islands with hot strangers I'm crushing on all the time.*

She patted the quilt as I stood there, dripping like an idiot.

"Now you know all about me," she said, "tell me all about you."

"Oh?" I asked. "What would you like to know?"

"Hmm," she mused, "let's start with a secret you've never told anyone before." I looked at her blankly. She continued, "Something about . . . desire."

Wow, she just went right for it, didn't she? I could feel my face flushing and I stammered for an answer, coming up with nothing coherent.

"Too broad a topic?" she interrupted. "Okay, let's start with this. Tell me about a love affair you had in college."

"Uh, okay," I said, "Sure. So, there was this girl." And then I proceeded to tell her all about Sarah. How we were roommates and one night she came into my room in the middle of the night and touched the small of my back and asked if she could climb into my bed. And how at first we just held each other and then we started kissing. And then later we fumbled around backstage before our band went on. And then after the show, sharing a cigarette out on the balcony, she felt me up and all these kids on the sidewalk below started hooting and hollering. I didn't think it was that interesting really, but the artist listened, bemused, a thin grin spreading on her face.

"It's sweet," she said. "I love the innocence of young queer love."

"Tell me about one of yours."

"Alright," she said with a sigh. "I was home for the summer from my second year of college, and we had an au pair staying with us, a woman who was living in the extra room in exchange for taking care of my mother's twins, who were fourteen years younger than me. My mother had me when she was just a child still, and I was a hellion, sneaking out all night and riding on the backs of boys' motorcycles. When the twins came along she was already rundown and needed a hand.

"This woman, Paulina, was slim and dark and beautiful and mysterious. And she and my mother didn't exactly get along. I mean, Paulina did what she was asked, but she didn't seem to like or respect my mother, and I'm sure she had her reasons. I don't know the whole story there. One night I stepped outside for a cigarette and I smelled weed. I followed it to Paulina, smoking a blunt under the apple tree.

"She offered it to me without a word, and I took it, and we got high. And then we were slunk down at the base of the tree and the sky was spinning with shooting stars and the musk of two lonely women with nothing to lose."

I smirked a little and the artist caught my eye. It sounded like a line she'd used before, and I started to wonder how many other women she'd seduced under this same tree with the same story.

"Don't believe me?" she asked.

I coughed. "Oh, no," I said, "go ahead."

"How about if I show you," she offered. "She was here." She patted the earth at the foot of the tree. "And I was here," she said, scooting over.

There we were, squished together in the shade, our bodies still wet, clothes stuck to us from the swim.

"Paulina reached up to touch my face," she explained slowly, as she brushed her fingers against my cheek, keeping her eyes level with mine. "And then . . ." she said, "I'm not going to tell you what happened next, because—"

"Because?" I asked, with a quiver in my voice.

"Because I want this to be original," she said.

There was a long pause.

I didn't care if it was a line or a story she'd used more than once. I'd been lusting after her for weeks, and now here we were, together, alone, like fucking Adam and Eve in the Garden of Eden.

"Do you?" she asked.

"What?" I breathed heavily, gasping a little for my senses.

"Do you want *this* to be original?" she asked.

"Yes," I said. Yes, I want this. Original. Now. All of it.

"Oh good," she said, as she leaned in towards me, "because I've been dreaming of it for a while now."

Come into Me

This piece explores feelings of safety and connection in the body, and may trigger strong emotions for some readers.

I AM COMING to you with gentle hands, lips, soft words, kindness, and an open heart. I am coming to you with this body, this attentiveness—I'm here for you. I'm all yours. You ascribe me any gender or age or specificities you want. I am here to witness you, to listen to you, to repeat what you say, to hold you, to bring you pleasure, to bring you back into your body, to help you feel safe. I am neutral. And you are safe. Whatever you say goes. Whatever you want is what we do. You control the narrative. And if you don't know what you need, just tell me that—and we'll figure it out together.

Yes, we can talk first. Yes, you can tell me everything that happened, even the things that are too horrible to say aloud or tell others who love you. Yes, I can hear all of it. Don't worry about me. Don't hold back. Tell me everything. It's important to say it aloud if you can. You won't hurt me by telling me. The truth needs to come out, that's part of how it will leave your body.

Yes, I will hold you. Yes, I will wipe your tears. Yes, I will give you space when you need it. Yes, I will listen to you say it over and over again if that's what you need.

This is not your fault. Nothing you did made this happen to you. You did not invite this. You did nothing wrong. This was not your choice. You did not initiate your pain. You did not okay it. You may not take responsibility for it.

Do you see my eyes? Do you see the kindness and acceptance in them? Do you see the love here? I see you as you are, as the whole you, the you of your entire life, and not just the you of what happened. This sorrow and pain are less than .1% of your life. You have lived 99.9% of your life in every other way. What fills you and makes you is the enormity of your existence beyond these wretched feelings. Every other day and night, each friendship and caring moment, every instance of joy and fun and delight and comfort makes you you. All these beautiful memories are within you, in your mind, your memory bank, your cells.

You feel a tear in the fabric of your life. It is big. It is terrible. It is awful. It is terrifying. It is the thing that makes everything feel different from now on. We can go on with a tear inside. We need to see it and recognize it and give it priority. When you are ready to patch, darn, or mend it, I am here to help you if you want me to.

I hear you saying this feels heavy in your body, like a weight blocking your path, obscuring your view. We are going to acknowledge that and work with it, and see if it feels right to shift it so that you can see around it again and won't feel trapped, maybe you'll even feel like it's gone and cleared out of your way. We can't change what happened. But we can change how you feel in your own body and psyche and soul. We can help you remember what normalcy and safety feel like, and we can bring that sensation back into your cellular memory.

I hear you saying you feel broken. I hear you saying you feel outside of yourself. I hear you saying you can't trust the world anymore, you can't trust people. That's all normal. That's all appropriate given what happened. Do you understand that? Your response is right on track. You are handling this as well as anyone could. You have to go through these stages to heal. You are still you. You are the same beautiful, unique, creative, thoughtful person you were before this moment in time, and you will continue to be that person, now, right in this moment, and in the future that unfolds into the rest of your life.

Can we use your imagination to help change the heaviness? Okay? So, let's try this. For just a moment, imagine seeing yourself in the future, at a time when you are smiling and carefree. Make eye contact with that future self. Ask that self if they're okay. Look into their eyes and ask, *Are you okay?* Let them tell you *yes,* and show you yes with their eyes, and let them show you yes with their body. Do they nod, do they twirl, or dance, or run, do they shoot a hoop, or walk down the street unafraid? See what they do. Ask them if you will feel okay again. When they tell you *Yes, you will be okay,* let that assurance come at you like a cloud of mist. It surrounds you. Step into that cloud, let the mist fill your body. Feel the coolness of it. Breathe it, let it replenish you, this new and different atmosphere, this change, this relief.

The mist feels like a rainforest. Let yourself enter this climate. It brings a sense of spicy ripeness, mystery, green voluptuousness, and wild growth. Let the climate become you. Your feet become the earth, thick with roots and dark soil. It is of you. You can sense it. You can smell the minerals. You feel anchored, grounded, and enriched in nutrients from all the little microprocesses of germination and transformation.

Shoots burst from seeds, plant matter decomposes into growing power, insects molt, and the honest degradation of the rotten becomes the renewed. You can feel all this in your body, just like in the soil, these small acts of metamorphosis. Let your body churn. Let anything clinging in your rainforest fall to this earth. Let it splat to the ground and donate its nutrients to your soil. The best soil comes from composted things. Let your belly, your lungs, your neck, your mouth, your ears, your eyes, all shed anything heavy or uncomfortable or stuck. Shake it loose. Give it all to the earth. Let it go.

What if we imagine in the soil of your pelvis a vine growing, and it symbolizes your pain. Does that feel okay? All right. Let's go with this metaphor. You can feel the vine thick and twisted throughout your pelvis. Its ropy branches are coiling through your torso, clenching your heart, and gripping your ribs and jaw. We are going to cut it down like the invasive weed it is and see and feel your body shed its grip. Ready?

See yourself sawing the stem. Hear the back-and-forth sound of the saw. The woody trunk of the vine is spitting sawdust and you can feel the creak and crack as it splits. See the vine lose its source of life. Watch the tendrils let go their grasp once their vitality is severed. Now let's fast-forward and bring in a little magic. The whole plant goes dry and flaky until the leaves fall lightly away and the whole vine, and every tendril of it, crumbles to dust. Back to the earth.

A sense of spaciousness fills you as the vine disappears. A calm, breezy, free sky kind of expansiveness. Can you feel that freedom inside? That openness? Breathe deep into your belly. Exhale loudly. Your heart and jaw and belly and lungs and ribs are free now.

Let's be thorough. We take our hands and we pull out the root. We extricate every last bit of the vine from you. Feel the vacancy in the soil there as a sense of peace, and imagine running your fingers through that dirt and how easily now they move through the loosened mineral-rich soil. Many ancient cultures have symbolized the earth as a Mother. Feel that divine feminine energy in your body. If you want to, you can plant a new tree here. Your favorite fruit tree, or any symbol of peace and tranquility and abundance, as a tribute to your body. Plant that seed in the soil of your pelvis, water it, say a blessing, and walk away to let it grow according to its own natural rhythms.

How are you feeling now?

Can you feel your feet on the floor? Can you feel your hands? Can you feel your face? Can you feel your skin as the edges of your body?

Your skin is the thing that separates you from the world. Your skin is your container. Your skin has little cells that act like drawbridges in a fortress. They allow or deny water, air, bacteria, micronutrients, and chemicals into your body. We don't know how to do their job. Only they do. Let's feel what a good job they are doing. No matter what you think about their efficacy, let's take a moment to be grateful for them and how hard they work. They might have an easier or a harder job based on certain circumstances, but no matter the conditions, we can trust they are working the best they are able and they deserve appreciation. Thank your skin. Thank your cells. Thank your entire body for the protective energy it gives you twenty-four seven without you even realizing.

Body, you are amazing. You are a natural wonder. You formed from practically nothing, to give me limbs and organs, a brain, and eyes and ears, a mouth and a soul, sensitivity and sentient awareness. Thank you thank you thank you.

You know that feeling you have when you admire someone? That glazed-eye look when you gaze upon a beloved? Put that look in your eyes right now. And now close your eyes and let that look seep into your head and flow through your body. Let your eyes flood your own body with that gaze.

Do you feel that?

Do you know how special you are?

Ask your body what it needs.

Does it want more words, some touch, a hug, something sensual?

It wants some sensual touch?

Okay, let's try that. We'll start slowly and see what feels good to you. If you feel a sudden "No" coming from your body, either before or during my touch, how would you most easily indicate that? You want to say "Stop"? Okay, I'll listen for that. I'll also be watching your face, and I'll check in with you if I start to see some hesitation or resistance, is that okay? Sometimes it's hard to say "Stop" or "No," and I want to be able to check in with you if I sense you might want to say it but are holding back.

First, I'm going to reach out and hold your hand.

Good, I'm glad that feels nice. I'm going to gently stroke your hand with my fingertips, okay? Up your arms too? Yes, gladly. I'm softly running my fingers down your arms. Can I kiss your palms? You have beautiful hands. When I bring them to my lips, your skin feels and smells so good. I can feel your good nature and your essence coming from your hands.

Yes, I'd love to hug you. Come here.

Your body is such a safe place for me. Your embrace feels wonderful.

Can I touch your neck?

Do you like my fingers running down your spine? I'm going to hold you tight while I keep doing that.

Yes, go ahead and cry. I've got you.

I've got you.

You'd like a kiss? Yes, of course, I'd love to kiss you.

You taste delicious. Your lips are so sweet. You feel so good in my arms.

Yes, I'll take you to bed, if that's what you want.

Take off your shirt? Like this?

You are stunning. Your skin gleams. You are such a beautiful individual.

What's that? Yes, let's stop. Let me hold you again.

Yes, go ahead, go to the bathroom, I'll be here. Take all the time you need.

Did you take a shower? Do you want me to, too?

No? Okay. Yes, I'd love to cuddle. I'm warm and dry.

You are so loveable. You are so loving.

You belong here. You belong in the world. Right now. Right here.

I don't know. I guess life has a bigger design than any of us can control or choose. Sometimes terrible things happen to wonderful people. I don't think there is any reason why. I don't think there's any way to understand it. Once I asked my meditation teacher why bad things happen, and they said they couldn't answer that question. "*Why* is not the question," they said. "Asking *Why* will only cause you suffering. The question is *What* do I do given these circumstances and *How* do I go on?" They told me that asking what to do and how to proceed empowers us to move forward. I guess getting caught up asking *why* paralyzes us, waiting for an answer that will never explain everything. My teacher reminded me that maybe what we need is guidance and support more than any explanation, especially if the questions aren't answerable. Does that resonate?

Would you like it if I kissed your neck?

Want me to run my fingers through your hair?

I feel your body pressing against mine. I feel your hips nesting into mine.

This feels like a yes, am I reading you right?

Yes, I'm taking off your underwear. Yes, I'm touching you lightly between your legs.

Yes, I feel your heat and smell your delicious scent and feel the silkiness of you.

Yes, you can touch me. Yes, you can rub against me and kiss me anywhere, everywhere.

Yes, I'll kiss your nipples. Yes, I'll lick your neck. Yes, I'll bring you pleasure.

Like this and like this and like this.

Come here. Come close. Come tight. Come strong. Come back.

Come back to yourself. Come back to me. Come back to us.

Yes yes yes yes.

I feel you all here. I feel your hands, your skin, your sweat, your breath, your lips—everything rich and full and wonderful and gorgeous. You are all here. You are so fucking amazing. You are so hot. And beautiful. And sexy. And rare.

I've got you. I've got you.

Let yourself come undone.

Let yourself start over from here.

From this point right here.

Reset button.

You are safe.

It feels so good to connect with you like this.

It feels so good to touch you like this.

Do you like that? More? More?

I'll give you more.

You like that. I love seeing you smile.

I love your hands pulling me closer. I love your kisses. You taste amazing. You are strong. You own it. This is your body. And it is an incredible body to witness. To touch. To be entwined with. You are stunning. You are sensual and scrumptious. I can feel you hot and throbbing. Let it pour out of you.

Everything from within you is pure beauty to me. Come on me. Come in me. Come into me. Let it flow. Feel my touch. Feel my body holding you. You like that? You like this? Yeah, you do. Oh yes. Oh yes. I've got you. More? More more. Yes yes yes.

Adam and Eve and All

HE WAS LYING on a pile of leaves and his leg was twitching. He was having a dream. The sun was playing shapes on his body, while the leaves above wrestled with the wind. Bodies of quick shifting light danced across his form, playfully tickling at his waist, his ribs. The sun cascaded over his small brown nipples. Light twisted its fingers through the soft, sparse hairs on his chest. A ribbon of warmth snaked down his neck, from his dimpled chin to his pretty collarbone, then suddenly shifted in a flash to his groin, kissed the flat valley of his belly, and disappeared, replaced by shadow.

The tree branches above him shook, resettled themselves, and leaned to see him better. His long brown body stretched out under the apple tree, dappled with light and shade, his dark lashes soft against his youthful cheeks, the crescent labyrinths of his ears quiet and still. The light ventured to his thighs, exploring the thick of them, and quickly scurried over the unusual fruits between his legs, two ripe figs and one shaped like the head of a snake. Adam moaned in his sleep and shifted slightly. A fuzzy caterpillar crawled along the ridgeline of his toes.

In the dream he was enveloped in light. He felt a softness around him, like being wrapped in a cloud. Something rippled past him as if the air had become water. He heard a murmur of music, the tumbling burble of the river, and a gentle voice calling his name. He saw a wash of auburn and a smear of bright blue. A color as green as the river flooded in.

Aaaaaah-daam, the voice cooed, and he felt a stirring inside him. Adam twisted his torso and his hand lifted in alarm, as if suddenly reaching for something, someone, and then, conquered by sleep, dropped limply across his chest. His fingertips rested on the wet earth, his palm warm against his ribs, his thumb just grazing his nipple. The ground lay scattered with apple seeds and yellow leaves.

The sun parted the branches of the trees and came to shine on Adam, bright and hot. The earth rolled beneath him, tilling a spatter of seeds into the soil. Adam's chest began to bulge, and in his sleep he whimpered.

In the dream, the voice called his name and the light went dark. He found himself bobbing in the river, splay legged and open-armed, with many arms and legs like some new kind of creature. He floundered in the water, spluttering for air.

A hand pressed up underneath the skin of his belly. Its shape was as clear as his own. Its index finger traced his rib line, from the inside.

The sun's long fingers pulled his skin apart, making an opening between the arches of his ribs, and while the earth rumbled beneath him, Eve came tumbling from his torso.

She lay slick and stunned beside him, stretched long in the arms of the sun.

The sun dried and warmed her, and then grew tired and went to rest.

All went dark, and the owl called for food with a screech and mighty flap.

Adam and Eve slept side by side under the bold moon perched like a curious parrot on a dark fold of the night sky.

In the morning, the sun stretched gloriously and colored everything pink.

Adam rolled onto his side, which was strangely sore, and sat up. He stretched and admired the morning sky as he always had—as long as he could remember. Which wasn't very long really.

He turned his head and was startled to see Eve, just opening her eyes and looking at him, or rather past him, but towards him. A flash of the dream came back to him—the swaddle of color, blue and auburn, a thick hold of clouds, tinkling sounds and a soft slip of motion.

Adam, she said.

Adam blinked and looked around him. Crocuses were pulsing a new growth out of the earth. A couple of grey-purple clouds hung low in the sky, rimmed in light, watching.

Adam bolted upright and clumsily stumbled to stand a bit away from Eve. He squinted at her, and marveled at how similar to him she looked, lying there under his favorite tree. The print of his body still pressed the leaves down in the shape of him next to her. He held his ribs, for fear he might fall apart.

Eve closed her eyes and tilted her head to the sky, wiggled her fingers and toes, and stretched her lean body long. She opened her eyes and studied the leaves layered on the tree, and the lines of tree limbs snaking through the canopy. Then Eve turned her eyes to Adam. She studied the sprigs of hair on his chest, the blunt curve of his nose, the little dancing line between his lips, the glimmer in his eyes. She then brought her fingers to her face and felt her eyes, her nose, her lips, all the while studying Adam. Adam stood, at once mesmerized and terrified. Eve placed her finger in her mouth and ran it along the ridge of her teeth. Her eyes widened when she discovered the soft creature of her tongue. She looked at Adam. Startled, he looked away.

Eve's hands met her body, and found every curve, every fold. Her fingers cupped the roundness of her breasts and rubbed the funny bump of her nipples. Surprised, she looked again at Adam. His gaze was fixed on her breasts and he would not meet her eye. Her hands kept moving. They smoothed over her waist and travelled her hips and circled her belly, where the skin was smooth and luscious. Her legs came together to meet at a delicate cleft between. Eve touched the little mound between her legs and ran her finger down the cleft. She swallowed and looked slowly around the garden with wondering eyes. She touched it again. The apples on the ground shuddered.

Then she moved on to her thighs and legs, the fronts of her knees and the backs of her knees, and her ankles and toes. She carefully inspected and caressed each toe. Adam gulped, watching her, and trying not to watch her. He looked at his own toes and wondered how it was he had never really noticed them much before.

Suddenly it all felt too much for Adam. He bolted like a gazelle and ran for the river.

Eve lay back down in the pile of yellow leaves, curious and groggy, and explored the texture of her hair with her hands. She petted her hair, her eyebrows, her eyelashes. She closed her eyes and felt the sun against them like a warm fingertip. She drifted back to sleep.

Adam plunged into the river and lay his body flat to the river-bed. The water rushed over him in a frenzy of white froth and sparkling currents. He felt the river scrambling around every curve of his body, the tiny slivers of it, glinting with sunlight, splintering his skin as they raced by. He opened his eyes and watched the sky, steady, behind the slippery tumult.

Adam rested on a rock in the sun and watched the water reflecting the leaves on the trees. Slashes of color fell into the water, and the water rippled them into different shapes. Here, the water was dark and deep and quiet. Adam leaned over to watch a small red leaf gliding, and there, he saw his reflection. Two eyes watched him, one nose, one wondrous mouth. Adam remembered Eve then—her hands, her eyes—and he touched his face.

His hand traveled to his cheek and there he paused, and blinked, and watched the shadows shifting in his face. He opened his mouth. He turned his head and stretched his neck. He stood up.

Adam saw his body shimmering in the shiny stretch of water. He turned his head delicately, raised his arms slowly over his head. He saw the muscles of his belly rippling as the water gently drifted. He touched his belly and felt the heat under his skin. He remembered Eve and moved his fingertips to his nipples. A current zipped through his body, like light shining through the leaves. Adam reached his hand down to the odd fruits dangling between his legs and felt a shift within him, a heat, a pull, a tightening. He thought of the wild wash of color from the dream. The image of Eve dappled in light in the yellow leaves flashed through his mind. He knew who she was then. She was *Eve.*

Eve lay under the apple tree, sleeping. Her dream was thick with textures and smells. She felt a silky softness in the palm of her hand, warm and ticking a fast little pulse. She smelled the rich scent of leaves baking in the sun, but stronger, a smell that created a surge within her, a long tug. Eve rolled her body belly-down to the earth and plunged her fingers into the earth, and the earth was hair, all hair, hair like her own. Her fingers tangled in it. She reached into the hair, deep down, past her elbow, and grasped something solid and small and round. She was lifting it up to the surface when she woke up. Adam was standing over her.

Adam's body carried the green scent of river rocks and a luminous gloss of water, which dripped from his hair onto Eve's shoulder. Adam appeared like a dark shape with a bright glint of light below his ear. The sun was setting behind him.

Eve, he said above her.

Eve's eyes fluttered as the stream of light rushed from behind Adam's ear to play in her lashes. She blinked and sat up, pressing her delicate fingers to the wet earth. Adam settled to the ground beside her and watched his own hand lift to brush the hair off her cheek. He marveled at the shape of her ear. He leaned in to inspect it and then turned his gaze to Eve's, who stared back. He touched her. His fingertips grazed the line of her eyebrow, slid down the side of her cheek. Her hand met his hand along the subtle arch of her collarbone, and there they rested, one hand upon another, and again their eyes met.

At that moment, Adam's fingertips were inscribed with whorls of knowledge. The softness and warmth of Eve's body wrote its way into him, and wove an imprint of pleasure into his skin. He learned what it was to learn. He learned that touch brings us more than we had before. He watched his hands run over her body as the river ran over the rocks. His hands ran the course her hands had run earlier that day. With each new curve and softness, Adam remembered her delicate fingers and let his hands mimic hers.

Grazing the full plumpness of her breasts, he exhaled a long breath laden with the aroma of apples. Eve wrapped her hand around his neck and drew him closer. He leaned into the smooth expanse of her belly and brushed his lips against her ribs. Eve reached her hand to his side, her palm warm as the sun. She held him there, where the skin was puckered and dark, like a chewed fruit. An owl hooted in the distance.

The way their bodies came together was spoken of forever after by the birds and the trees and the apples and the sun. And a new immediacy coiled through the garden, craving such fervent intimacy. Every rustle and stretch of growth now laced with a murmur of desire. Trees wished they could grow closer together and tried. They hitched up their roots and scooted near, their limbs slowly and deliberately growing to entangle one another's. The apples loosed their suckered hold off the branch and fell deftly, thrilling to spill their seeds on impact, to mingle their rotten pulp on the ground. The birds chattered the story endlessly, and it transformed and rolled and shifted, as told stories do. How four hands touched two bodies. How they became a strange creature of arms and legs and limbs, a twisted thing of two heads, double-spined, and rolling. How the trees lifted their branches and gawked. And the roots in the ground beneath them shivered.

And how on that day, the sun hovered over the horizon, stalling, aggravating the impatient moon.

Drummer Grrl

WE WERE ALL sweaty and wild-eyed when our favorite punk riot grrl band, Trousers, finished their set. My heart was pounding especially hard after watching their new drummer bang it out in every song. Geez, those biceps. And the way their sweaty hair kept thrashing in the air and sticking to their cheeks in long sharp strands. The force they used to pummel the drums, the velocity, the intensity, the passion. I had to introduce myself. I roamed through the bar, making my way through the sweaty crowd. The vanilla smell of dry ice floated through the air alongside the verdant funk of lit doobies and the thick tang of armpits. Where was the striking androgynous drummer with the strong arms?

Holly and Tracy were out back passing around a little gold flask with the lead singer, Megan, who was shivering in a faux fur coat and platform heels. We greeted each other and huddled together against the cold, praising the band and Megan's performance while watching our breath puff into the night air under the streetlights. I tried to ask casually who the new drummer was, but they caught on right away. I can spot a babe in an instant, and everyone knows that about me. I got a few elbows to the ribs.

"Yeah, she goes by Chay," Megan informed me, "and I think I saw her head backstage after our set."

"Do you know if she's, um, single?" I asked.

Megan shrugged and smiled. "Why don't you go ask her?"

I excused myself, imaging that they started placing bets on the likelihood of Chay turning me down the moment I left. I headed back into the club and wandered around behind the stage. There were a lot of cute people milling about, but none as compelling as Chay. Where was she? I hoped she hadn't left.

I was running out of options for where to look, but I couldn't give up. I went out to the parking lot and scanned for any stragglers. There she was—sitting on a high ledge talking on the phone. I didn't know what to do. Should I back away, pretending I was looking for someone else, estimate how long her phone call would take, and then come back and hit on her? Why do I always feel like such an idiot when I like someone? I stood there trying to decide what to do, and miracle of miracles, Chay caught my eye and smiled. I smiled back. She waved and pointed to the phone. I nodded and stood there, frozen, wondering if that meant she actually wanted to talk to me, or if, in the dark, she had me mixed up with some other lookalike dyke.

She hung up, hopped down from the ledge, and walked over.

"Hi," she said.

"Hi," I said. "I loved your set."

"Thanks."

We smiled, and kinda checked each other out.

"I'm Mel. She/her."

"Nice to meet you, Mel. I'm Chay. She/her. I saw you in the crowd."

"Really?" I grinned. "I was pretty into your drum skillz, couldya tell?"

Chay laughed. "That's cute." she said.

"Really," I insisted. "I was mesmerized. Your face is unforgettable. And, um, I really like your arms."

"Hey," Chay said, "It's really cold out here. Wanna go inside?"

"Yeah," I said, "let's."

As we headed inside, I brushed my fingers against her elbow. Any excuse to touch her arm.

"I know a little place," Chay said, guiding me through the crowd to this door that opened to a narrow stairwell.

"Go ahead," Chay insisted, and I climbed up into a small attic nook tucked above the bar. It was a slanted triangle of a room, a corner of finished loft space, strung with holiday lights and made cozy with a little velvet loveseat and a few beanbag chairs atop a striped rug. No one could see us in here.

"This is cool," I whispered in the dim glow of the rainbow lights.

"Yeah, it's a secret," Chay whispered back.

"Ohmigod, you're so cute," I blurted out. "So hot, I mean, uh, more so than cute. I mean both, but, damn, really hot." I was stumbling, correcting myself, and Chay was laughing.

"Mel, relax. I think you're cute and hot too." She paused. "Look, I don't know where this is going, but just letting you know, I'm trans."

"Oh," I said. "Thanks for telling me." We looked at each other. I got closer. I took her hand.

"Anything you wanna tell me?" she asked. Chay held my gaze with gleaming eyes.

"I would love it if you kissed me," I breathed.

Chay leaned in, cupped my head, and kissed me with warm, full lips. It was a deep kiss, insistent and sensual, my favorite kind. I kissed her back, and we pressed together, our arms feeling each other's backs and necks and shoulders, moving down to the waist, the ass. I pressed my hips to hers, and she held my waist back for a second, then circled her arms around me and cinched me tight. My mouth found her neck, her ear, her collarbone. We sank into a beanbag and made out in a frenzy, squishing it this way and that. I could hear the next band starting up—a wailing singer, jagged electric guitar, and thumping base keyboard.

Chay and I couldn't get enough of each other. We grabbed, rolled, wrestled, giggled, tackled, and ground against each other.

"I want you," I breathed into her ear.

"Do you want to talk about consent?" she offered, freeing her mouth for a moment.

"No," I panted, pouncing atop her.

We both laughed.

"I consent, I consent, I consent," I whispered between kisses.

"To what? To what? To what?" she mocked, between kisses.

"Tell me if I'm too much, okay?" I asked, licking her neck.

"You're not too much. I'll let you know what I want and don't want, don't worry about that." She spoke in a sultry voice, bringing her hands to the waist of my shirt, and looked into my eyes to wait for an answer. I nodded, letting her know she could lift it off.

"Yours?" I asked. She shook her head. "Okay," I said, putting her hand on my breast.

While Chay caressed my breasts, she began to kiss all along my bra line, from one strap to the next, licking down my cleavage. I shivered. She then returned to each nipple to breath warm air onto them and nip them a little with her lips. I groaned and ran my fingers through her hair.

"Can I kiss your belly?" I asked.

Chay lifted her shirt up and I went in. She smelled like the best kind of sweat, like spice and musk, an aroma I couldn't get enough of. I wanted to roll around in it like a dog rolls in the grass. Her skin was exuding this heady fragrance from every pore, after all that sweaty drum exertion. Her scent was ambrosia. I kissed the arches of her ribcage down to her waist and then licked across her waist, tugging on the skin, licking the jut of her hipbones, and basically going down on her belly button. She liked it. Her breathing got ragged as she gyrated her hips. My tits rubbed between her legs and I could feel the steamy energy between the two of us building. I licked all the way across her belly at the rim of her jeans.

"Chay," I breathed, "What do you want?"

She pulled me up so that I straddled her lap. I could feel her hard, hot, and pulsing under her jeans, and I couldn't help it, I just sighed this weird moan and collapsed a little in my lust. My body got heavy and I started rocking my hips to her lap, rubbing our junk together through our clothes. I looked into her eyes. They glinted in the dark.

"Sorry," I said. "I'm listening."

She smiled.

"I got distracted," I drawled.

"This feels nice," Chay said, "keep doing that."

I put Chay's hands on my hips so she could steer me faster or slower, and so she could lift me a little if she needed to as a signal that I was pressing too hard. But once her hands were on my hips, she just rocked me harder and faster, her strong-as-fuck biceps pumping, a determined look on her face, like when she was playing the drums. Her eyes got sharp and her mouth drew into a line. It was the friction, the intensity, the surprise, the passion, her muscles, all of it, but then her face, that look on her face, that made me come, in a great heaving extended pulsating rhythmic gasp that just went on and on and on. When I couldn't keep going any longer, I collapsed on Chay and we lay there, catching our breath.

"Fuck," I said, once I could finally speak.

"Yeah," she confirmed, holding my head and patting my hair.

For some reason that made me burst out giggling.

My face was in her armpit. "Um, we are gonna smell entirely like cum when we go back down there and see our friends."

"True," Chay said, "but I think the night is young, yeah?"

"Yeah," I agreed, lifting my head to kiss her. "Chay," I asked, "Can I go down on you?"

"Mm, I'd love that," she said, "but let's take a little break and talk first."

We adjusted ourselves, sweaty and disheveled, and rested our backs against the base of the loveseat. She held my hand.

"So, I have a steady. And we have an open relationship," Chay informed me.

"Oh, okay," I said.

"And . . . he is who I was talking to on the phone."

"Oh . . ."

"I told him there was someone cute at the show and I wanted to make sure he was okay if I hooked up with someone tonight. And . . . that someone is you. I didn't wanna make assumptions, but I had my eye on you, and I wanted to know if it was okay to make a move. We don't have to ask each other permission, but we are super considerate and we do check in. That's part of our deal."

My mind was blown. Chay had noticed me during the show. I'd thought she just said that in the parking lot because that's what hot drummers say to their fans. I had no problem with her being in a relationship. And I was into her transparency.

"Yeah, that's amazing. I mean, that's really cool that you two communicate so well. I don't know what to say. I'm flattered?"

Chay laughed. "So, you're okay with this being a hook-up and maybe just for tonight?"

"Yeah," I exclaimed. "That's okay with me. This is like the funnest surprise ever, to have this sexy clandestine encounter with you." I gestured to the attic nook.

"Do you get tested?" she asked.

"Yeah, I do. I was just with one other person since my last test, but I don't worry about that, there was really no risk with what we did. Do you?"

"Yeah, we are pretty careful. I mean not, like, scrupulous, but, again, considerate."

"Do you feel okay about this? If we go further?" I asked.

"Yeah, I do," she said, playing with my hand, and fondling my fingers. "You?"

"Uh huh," I mumbled as I kissed the beautiful ridge of her shoulder where her shirt had slipped down.

"So, wait," I stopped. "You noticed me in the audience?"

She nodded.

"And then what did you think when I showed up awkwardly in the parking lot?"

"I figured you'd felt my energetic beckoning. That you'd received my *qi-mail*," she laughed.

"You are truly amazing," I murmured. "You goddess."

Chay giggled. "Come here."

More making out on the rug, on the beanbag, on the loveseat. I sat her down, straddled her and rode her some more, biting her ear and cuffing her shoulder with my hand.

Once we caught our breath again, I slid to the floor and put my hand on her fly.

"Yes or no?"

"Yes," Chay murmured.

I unbuttoned and unzipped, keeping my eyes locked on Chay's. I slid her jeans over her ass and ran my fingers over her tight striped skivvies. I put my head in her lap and inhaled. "It's crazy how good your body smells. I've never smelled someone so delicious."

"You are such a charmer," Chay teased.

"Seriously," I said, "it's unreal. You're rocking some top-notch pheromones."

When I rubbed and kissed her through the fabric, she moaned and tipped her head back. After a while, I eased her skivvies down her legs and slid them off. I spread her legs and ran my hands up her thighs, teasing her taint, her ass cheeks, and her shaft with soft, sensual fingers. Tucked in her head was a Prince Albert piercing.

"Wow," I murmured before licking it.

"Yeah," she sighed, "The dream of the 90s is alive in my clit." I took her into my mouth. Chay groaned.

"Mmmm," I moaned, thrilled to engulf her. Chay arched her ribs and pressed herself into me.

A genital in the mouth becomes the essence of eros: carnal, plump, fluid, juicy, steamy and springing, savory, salacious, and throbbing in its aphrodisia.

When Chay and I fucked, I dissolved into shapelessness, into a glittering wanton state. We met there, in a slippery alter-reality of lust, longing, and letting go, lolling in our mouthwatering lechery.

"Do you want this?" I asked, my finger on her asshole.

"Yes," she affirmed. I spit on my finger and slid it inside her, crooked and probing. Her ass felt amazing, so tight and sweet.

"Fuck me," Chay insisted as I sped up my rhythm.

Chay was squirming, with little sobs escaping her lips. She whispered harshly, "Make me be more quiet. But—don't stop!"

I clasped my other hand over her lips and felt the hot wet slit of her mouth bump against my palm as I fucked her.

Her asshole puffed up inside, getting plumper and plumper, and it was turning me on to the extreme. My mouth kept sucking her, tasting the flavors of our passion. Chay came hard with smothered gasps and a suppressed bellow. I fell on top of her and she kissed me hungrily. Her hands made quick work taking off my pants, and she pushed me to my knees. Soon she'd slipped a finger inside, her palm thwacking my clit as she fucked me. She took a nipple into her mouth and grabbed my ass with her other hand. I fucking love being taken. And Chay was indeed taking me. She was taking me to the places I wanted to go, to the melty outer space place that we had touched together all night.

"More!" I growled, and Chay put two more fingers inside me. She widened them to make her hand thicker, and kept the rhythm so good, pounding into me. I could tell she could go all night. Nothing beats getting fingered hard by a drummer.

"More," I begged, and Chay caught my drift, inserting her pinky and working her way to get her thumb in, then easing her whole hand in carefully as she kept the rhythm. She kept checking in with her eyes, watching my face and waiting for me to nod.

"Fuuuuck" I grunted as Chay fisted me and I lost my mind a little. Tits flopping, my bare ass hanging out, pussy drool running heavy down my thighs.

"Come all over my hand, Mel," Chay purred, coaxing an orgasm out of me. I lost the sensation of her hand inside me. The pounding vaporized. All I could feel was my cervix going electric, a glowing inside and lift-off sensation like a UFO buzzing into the sky.

"Ohhh, ohhh, ohhh," I gasped as I came in a cosmic kind of way, with sensual delight spilling from within the very core of my body. My nipples lit up like Christmas lights. I could feel the ripples of the orgasm pooling inside each elbow and knee. I could feel the shock waves of it in my teeth.

Chay slowed and slowed her fucking, as my pussy clenched and released and clenched and released her hand. Every cell in my body had melted and was tingling. It took me a while to come back. Once everything settled and stilled, she pulled out carefully and laid her hand on my belly while I rested. She curled up next to me.

"You are a marvel," she said.

"Takes one to know one," I said.

"So much fun," she murmured.

"This was a hell of a chance encounter," I replied.

"Yeah," she agreed, laughing.

"So, am I, like, your hot fan girl one-night stand?" I asked, batting my eyelashes.

"Yeah," she said, "this drummer grrl saw you in the crowd and said, 'I pick that one.' And here we are."

"Here we are." I sighed and rolled over, reaching for my pants. "This was amazing. Thank you." I looked in her eyes. "Sincerely."

"My pleasure to share such pleasure with you, fan girl."

"This was a night I will not forget. Rock on, drummer grrl."

Licked Chrysalis

MOUTH TO MOUTH, we become something other than ourselves. Your tongue enters this wet cavern of mine like pink taffy stretching and stretching. It is its own creature, like the proboscis of some insect. I feel it snaking under my palate, dodging my uvula, shimmying down my throat. I'm moaning and creaming my shorts, held captive by its muscular allure. It has a mind of its own, savage. I can feel the willful muscle of your tongue rim my heart with a sultry lick as it shimmies down my gullet. I shiver with nipple rising pleasure and feel faint. How have I not fallen down? Some other mythical presence must be holding me up. Ah yes, I feel it, like fingers on my ribcage. I have sunk into a standing chair—does my spine work? I can't feel my legs.

My skin starts to itch and I break out in a sweat. My vision has gone blurry. Oh, now it's turning kaleidoscopic. Everything is a mandala shimmering with light. My shoulders feel bubbly, like something is starting to prickle beneath my skin. A crinkly sound surrounds me. Echoes in a cave. What is this ecstasy?

Your tongue rolls through me, like a cunning creature romancing my insides. Crepusclar, it becomes even more alive within me—a seductress in the dark. Slipping around my hip bones, trickling down my legs to graze the arches of my feet. It's sucking on the insides of my toes. Oh my word.

Your tongue is filling me with some kind of potion. This slick wet muscle is exuding a chemical as it explores my insides with its sensual charm. I'm under a spell. My vision is prismatic. I see bursts of light in geometric patterns shimmering with rainbows. I feel lit with color inside, dazzling rays of bliss. My organs are being fondled, caressed, and rearranged, dripping with this pheremonic mystery.

There is no part of me left untouched by your slim, long tongue. Its nature is playful and more sensual than anything I've ever felt. What's this? Your tongue is now coiling in my pelvis. I feel it sliding like a serpent around and around. Oh, oh, oh! I feel it licking my g-spot from the inside. Ohhhhh, I can't. I've never.

I'm gushing! This flood. The licking. The gland fills so fast. It's bulging, bulging, brimming. I'm flooding again. My pelvis is drowning, lost in a sea of my own juices. Antennae burst from my forehead. My mouth sprouts its own sticky tongue. There's that otherworldy feeling again, the tongue licking me inside out, and I'm filling, full, bursting, dissolving. I deliquesce, I am lost, I am lost in it, I am bright, I am electric, I am born.

Sacrilicious

MY SEXY SEMITIC sister—who is not actually my sister, but the widow to my late brother—is also my secret lover. We share a whispered sisterhood. Because of our black curls. Because our tongues were born dripping with oil and honey. Because our skin tastes like salt and the sun-kissed fields, and our cunts are fragrant like freshly churned butter. Because we are the new sisterhood, the old sisterhood, and the ancient sisterhood, the survivors, and everything in between. Because we are divine. Because we hold secrets. Because we are golden.

Sister in Hebrew is *achot*. Girl, you put the "hot" in *achot*. Come closer, let me smell the roses in your hair. Feel me running honeysuckle over your wrists, your breasts, your hips. I'll lick the pollen off of every inch of your glorious skin. Let me decorate you. This little blossom rests right here in your navel. The aroma wafts between us, up to you, and down to me. I inhale it while I kiss your belly and make my way to your bush, heaven sent, gorgeous and lush, sultry with your spicy fragrance. I can feel how slick you are. I can feel your hips roll like the ocean wanting me. I want you that bad too, my love. I wanna roll you into my ocean.

Where did you get these gorgeous deep brown eyes from, achot? From your aba, your ema, your bubbe? This golden skin, these black ringlets, these perfect lips.

How did you get these magnificent breasts? These heavy pendulous perfections with the conical dark nipples like candies I want to savor. I can't take my mouth off you. I want to drink you like wine.

Your body is sacred. Your mouth is a treasure. I want your nectar every night.

We meet in the river when no one is looking. I run my fingers down your hips, lift you up and hold you in my arms, so that I can suckle your nipples and run my tongue into your armpits. You toss your head back, your hair tumbling like a black waterfall down your elegant back. Under the cover of a willow tree, I cradle your ass like a grand basket lifted from the water, and move you up and down in my arms so that our clits rub together in delicious friction. My feet are bare on the silty river bottom, and I can feel the muck seeping away beneath my soles. But I won't stop. I won't stop until you arch your back and cry out, emitting that howl of an orgasm that sounds like a wild beast stalking some innocent prey in the night.

You let loose from me, grab my hand, and we scramble up the riverbed. We hide under the quince tree with the bell-shaped branches, and you place my hands against the trunk. "Stay!" you whisper harshly. I feel your hands press my feet into the dirt and pull my ass away from the tree toward you. Smack! You slap my bottom with your lovely hand. Thwack! You slap me again on the other side.

I feel you slide behind me to crook my ass in your belly, and then your knee is up under my pussy rubbing back and forth. My cunt lips respond right away to that. You knew they would. I feel them warm and puff up, glistening. Soon there is a slipperiness on your grinding thigh, and you glide faster. I feel my legs go weak so I grip the tree trunk. Your hands press my wrists and grip them there while you move faster and faster. When I gasp, you release my hands, press your fingers into my mouth, and extract them with my spit.

You slip your hand into the valve between my legs and hook it there while you shimmy your arm. You know this drives me wild. I begin to moan like a savage thing. No one can hear us. The entire shtetl is asleep, except for Moira the crone, and we all know any vibration of sex she picks up consciously or unconsciously is good for her and blesses her lonely soul and she'd never tell. So, we keep going.

G-d is good, g-d is good, I mumble under my breath, while getting gloriously fucked by you, my sister-in-law, under the fruit tree. Rotten quinces ferment in the earth beneath me. I slip on their pulp and seeds as I struggle to stay standing against the oceanic wave building inside me. *Ohh ohhh ohhh*, I sing like a prayer, as the sensation floods me. My pussy clamps around your hand in spasms and won't let go. You won't stop. You keep going, pumping your slender fist into my cavern, while kissing each rung down the ladder of my spine. My womb spasms again, as I crouch in a paroxysm of pleasure. I can feel cum dripping down my legs like syrup. When you stoop down to lick it up, running your tongue up my ankle to the back of the knee, I shiver and sigh. This is our Garden of Eden, right here. Sacrilicious.

Other nights, we meet at the edge of the field, where the grain is easily pressed to a bed. Where we can kiss and hold each other all night long and breathe each other in, along with the warm aroma of millet, long toasted all day in the sun, seeping its fragrance all through the night, just like we do. I meld with your deep brown love. We kiss noses, cheeks, ears, lips, the corners of mouths. And when we sleep, we fit one inside the other. Your eyelashes bat against my shoulder. Your breath is a soft breeze behind my ear. Our bodies entwined in the moonglow is a revelation. I long to sculpt a replica of us from clay. To draw the slippery mud from the river and craft it with my hands into a semblance of you and me. Beautiful you. The shape of us.

At dawn we rise and return to the village. Our spot would appear to have held a family of deer through the night. And who wouldn't think otherwise? Who would guess two women as good as us would become such amorous beasts under the moon? Nobody knows but our Shechinah and the stars. They saw it all and they were twinkling.

Drown the Patriarchy

TODAY I JERKED off by imagining squirting all over the patriarchy and drowning them to death. How could one woman have enough pussy juice, you might ask? Oh, I do. Trust me. In my fantasy, all the itty-bitty shitty politicians are gathered together as if for a fireworks display. The image of me, my body, my vibrator, my wet-as-fuck pussy, is projected into the night sky like a gigantic hologram. They all think they're getting the peep show of their lives. I can't see them. I can only see my lover standing before me here, naked, and hungry to fuck. They see my cunt above them, large and luminous against the black. And I am an erotic supernova of divine feminine power.

They want my pussy so bad. They're straining for it, standing on their little tiptoes, their ugly calves all buckled. They wouldn't even know what to do with it if they could reach it, would they? They are just pulled to the magnet of it. My pussy taunts them. Her rage shudders the sky. Her crown of mighty pubic hair is radiantly explosive, and she disappears and reappears, as if the circuits are loose, as if to say, you aren't reliable, well neither am I!

Watching my pussy's unleashed fury, my lover is getting very excited, and very handsy, which amps up my passion. The shitty politicians are growing more confused and dumbfounded, mesmerized by my vulvanova, which is draining the power right out of them.

Not one of them can get it up. My matriarchy is stealing their mettle. They are no match for me. Because they don't get to take control now. Because I come like an avalanche when I am this turned on. Because I am the motherfucking weather. And I will hurricane them out of office.

It's getting stormy. My lover is talking dirty. But they don't know that. They can't hear us in my own private space. All they see is my cam image up in the sky. They have no idea what's coming. They don't understand that when we goddesses get turned all the way on, we flood. They missed that opportunity. Never made a woman come? Well, maybe in the next lifetime, sucker!

Lemme tell you something. When a pack of self-righteous entitled shithead liars like these fellows dies by pussy juice, guess what? They get reincarnated as kind-hearted people. Really. God just told me. God is whispering in my ear. And she is on our side. When each of these evil souls gets transformed, they will be turned into a nice little baby feminist raised by lesbians and gays and trans folks. That's reality, we live in a dualistic world, and that's how it works. What goes around comes around. Oppress much? You won't in the next lifetime!

All of these thoughts on redemption and reincarnation and restorative justice are turning me on. I've got my eye on my lover and those meatsacks have their eyes on me. Oh, I'm getting so hot thinking about all those parents gleefully fucking in the New Matriarchy while their sweet little babies sleep peacefully in their cradles, resting until they are old enough to discern injustice and fight like hell to make the world a better place.

My lover is doing amazing things right now, and oh, what was just whispered in my ear, I can't even repeat. I feel the energy building, oh god, my whole body is starting to tingle, I'm fucking myself deep and long and thick, and my lover is getting in on the action, making me more turned on than I ever thought I could be. It's coming, oh god, it's coming. I'm coming. The rain is starting to fall, Oh god, oh god. I'm gushing, I'm gushing. I've never flooded this much, it's bottomless!

It's an astronomic amount of fluids dumping out of the sky. They're having to swim. The ones who had their mouths open when it happened are choking. You better choke on me, you shithead! I'm coming again, I'm coming, I'm coming, I'm coming! I. Cant. Stop. Coming.

It's a hurricane, Category 5, the swell is so deep, they can't escape. They're drowning. Bald heads like little floating golf balls. Toupees are gonna clog the storm pipes! We don't care. We'll deal with it later!

Oh god, one more time, just for good measure, I'm commmmmminggggggggggg. Ohhhh!

It's so good. It's so deep. It's so wet. It feels so fucking good. My whole body is quaking. The whole galaxy is shifting, the stars are rearranging, it's a new era!

We've washed them all away.

We've refreshed every ocean on the planet. Whales that were once extinct are coming back. Look, there's a dolphin pod! And they're singing! The world has been born anew. And all these old dickrags are history, drowned and washed away, food for the fishies.

Windows (Three Tableaux)

I

You see the hill of her hip lit by lamplight, a burst of earth
cooled by the breath of the moon.

The windowpane boxes her landscape into a composition, a bell
curve within a square.

She is held.
Here, in the square.
Here.

Her hip shifts, a subtle undulation,
catching the lamp glow and tugging its line like a ball of yarn.
Light tumbling down a hill.

The echo of her exhale flutters in her skin.

The air shifts around her, darkness washing through light.
Air takes shape, rippling around the curve of her body.

As the earth gears for a seism—
Roll tumult heave. Spasm. Rolling rolling rolling.

Some lift lifting, a push, towards a great unfolding.

For her it is
Fingertips. Breath. The wet stamen of a tongue. The coaxing caress of touch. More. Less. Lighter. Lightwaves. Heatwave. Heat.

Sunrise. Full sun. Blinding.
Her body rolls with the motion of land mass. Hills sink. Valleys
shift. The shadow sweeps in.

And now her face and torso in the windowpane. Her mane of
hair.

Her mouth shifts open, loosening its horizon line. The white
edge of her teeth suspended in that dark hollow. I can see her
breath coming hard now. Her eyes roll up, the delicate ridges of
her cheeks drop, her chest rises and falls in quick pulses like a
bird.

The air is charged with static. The air is hitting the window glass.

Her body jolts like she hit the glass. But, no, she is there, her
mouth in a cry. Her eyes blindly open. Chest quaking. Inside
her something unrolling unrolling unrolling.

Her fingers tracing the line of light that runs down her breast.
The delicate break as the line leaps at the nipple. The tender
swell at her belly. Her lashes close to her cheek.

II

Rough body to body. Prickly hair friction. The ceiling fan spinning. Wave after wave of cool air swashing.
The backs of hands held tight to the bedspread.

A face kisses from the light.
The clink clink of the ceiling fan as the bobble switch hits the
light fixture over and over.
Breath in juts and gasps.
Glasses clinking in the other room. Laughter. Hush now. Come
now.
Somewhere beyond the noise swell the static hush of the ocean.
A body red rubbed raw.
Finger curl, locked in the sheet.
A face framed in the box of the pillow.
It is smeared like a painter took a comb to its thick clotted
surface.
Francis Bacon raking his devious fingernails through the paint-
ed one portraited there on the bed. His thick hands pawing the
image of her face. His breath blowing the paint dry.
Her body is luminous with a shine of sweat.
Her nipples firm and tall.
Her toes curled like cooked shrimp.
The long lines of her legs are obscured by broad shoulders.
The sheets around her body like a tangle of grass.
The ocean breathing at the window.

There will be a brush taken to her wrist, her elbows, her thighs.
A brush recreating the long slope of her neck, a raw red line.

The night wild beyond these walls, this box.

The sky spinning so fast it looks like it is resting, it looks still.

A whirlpool that could suck you away in an instant—
if you could only reach through to touch it.

III

There's a way to surrender, to release this tight hold. This net woven under the surface of skin, there's a way to unlock it. Basket stretch, elastic pull, open weave. I want to unravel. Take this string and pull. Undo me.

Hold me like this. Touch me like this. Put your fingertips here.

Release me.

Talk to me.
Get me to soften.

I want pleasure.

Pleasure on the other side of the wall. On the other side of my hand. On the other side of my skin. Pleasure in your breath beat. Pleasure in your salt scent. Pleasure in the rhythm of our bodies as they hit hit hit.

I want it to wash over me like a wave, take me by the waist and pull me down, drown me.

Drown me.

That pleasure in me.

That pleasure filtering through me like light glittering in steam.

It is after pleasure that my earth shifts.
My landscape has changed.
There is a new chasm, a new rift. An openness that wasn't there

before.
A feeling of flying.
An unimpeded freedom—
like that gasp you feel upon seeing the Grand Canyon for the
first time.
All that space,
what is it?

Bifurious (Part Three)

IT STARTED WITH a text.

> Last Sunday was [flame emoticon x3]
> What you got going on later this week?
> You + me?

I had been wondering when the boyfriend would contact me. I had thought about asking him out, but I decided I wanted him to make the move. I was the newest member of the foursome and I didn't want to ruffle any feathers by asserting solo time with the one member I hadn't been with alone yet. Ha, *member*, I snorted. He had a gorgeous cock, and it was made crystal clear to me that night when I was in the tub with the wife, and he was pulverizing the husband's cranny, that he was skilled in the sack. I wanted to try him on for size.

I had been with the husband in the pool hall, the wife in the bathtub, and now it was time decide on a place to fuck the boyfriend. Where could we go? Not to my apartment. Too boring. Not to his . . . too intimate. Was there somewhere in public we could fuck? Maybe a locker room or a sauna? Nah, too risky. It came to me then. I wanted the boyfriend outdoors, with the night air streaming in, a gearshift pressed to my thigh. I wanted a good old-fashioned car fucking. I hadn't had one of those since high school.

I suggested he pick me up at eight and take me to his favorite bar. It sounded classic, sophisticated, and bossy. I wanted him to see me that way. Obviously, he went for bossy women, I mean look at the wife. I enjoy dominating a man, I just don't do it often. I'm so quick to roll over and submit. But, somehow, I knew instinctively I wanted to dominate the boyfriend. It was just a thing I couldn't get out of my mind.

He rolled up in an old Toyota pickup, and as soon as I got in I could tell he was wearing cologne. He doesn't know me well enough to know that I can't stomach cologne. I really wish I could, I have nothing against it, personally, but my body rejects it wholly. I get a headache and nauseous, I can't concentrate, and I can't get it out of my nose. It feels like the nasal equivalent of someone shining a flashlight in my eyes, the way it invades my senses so harshly. After we greeted each other, I settled into the passenger seat uneasily and announced, "You're gonna have to wash that off."

"What?" he asked.

"Your cologne."

"Oh, does it bother you?"

"Yes. I'm embarrassed to say, I can already feel a headache coming on. I don't know why for the life of me I'm so sensitive to fragrances, but I am."

"I have an idea," he said. "Hang tight."

He tooled the truck around and we headed in the opposite direction, careening through the woods skirting the town, zipping down roads parallel to pretty little streams, and finally rambling over a long bridge and pulling in to the driveway of a waterside cabin. It was the golden hour, and the sun was like low fruit fiercely clinging to the sky, blazing with effort. Everything was still and quiet and radiant. The water gleamed with sharp, wavering golden lines.

"I'll buy you that drink later, if you like, but this is our new first stop," he said with a grin.

Chivalrous, he opened my door and held out his hand.

"This is my friend's summer home, and I have an all-access any-time pass to come here." He led me around the grounds. "There's an outdoor shower, a dock to jump off if we want to swim, and some out-door lounge chairs." It was beautiful, so serene and private. "No bar though," he laughed.

I refused him a smile, trying on the role. "Shower first," I demanded, pointing a harsh finger at him, "with *lots* of soap." I gave him a look like he'd been a naughty boy to wear that cologne. "And then we swim."

He shuffled over to the shower, his head hung low.

"You go," I ordered. "I'll watch."

The boyfriend was sheepish. He began to unbutton his shirt, looking up at me with a hangdog expression. I assumed the face of a disgruntled schoolmarm.

His chest was hairy and his shoulders nicely sculpted. He had a few tattoos I hadn't been able to see in the firelight that night when I was in the next room getting bathed and deliriously screwing the wife. When he undid his pants, his cock tumbled out half-hard. Not bad. Quite lovely, really. His cock was thick and veiny with an uncircumsized tip. He awkwardly hopped to remove his pants and underwear and stepped aside to turn on the water, standing a few feet off until it warmed. He grinned and then responded to my stern expression, wiping the grin off. His face faded to a wide-eyed blank look. It was an act, and he was a mediocre actor. I could see a little secret smile hidden in his cheeks.

"I want to see that soap foam," I barked at him. I was fully clothed, standing a few feet away with my hands on my hips.

He slathered up and rubbed the soap suds all over his body with his hands. He ran it through his hair and washed it thoroughly, his head tipped back, eyes closed, Adam's apple sharp in his neck. His nipples were tiny, dark, and hard. He ran his sudsy hands all over his chest, his waist, his ass, and down between his legs. He soaped his chunky prick and glanced up at me to make sure I was watching as he suggestively stroked it.

"Uh-uh," I ordered. "Just wash."

Chastised, he returned to his task of soaping up again and running the suds all over his body for a second time. Again, the hair, rubbing more and more soap over his neck and jawline and shoulders. He was enjoying me watching, I could tell.

"Rinse it off," I said coldly.

He bent his fingers and started to scratch his neck. Then he filled his palms with water and slathered it all over his neck and chest. He rinsed languorously, trying every so often to catch my eye. Finally, he turned the water off.

"Will you tell me if the smell is gone?" he asked meekly.

I jerked one finger to indicate he could step out. He stood there shivering like a wet dog while I approached him shrewdly and sniffed around. Thank goodness I couldn't detect the perfume anymore.

"You've satisfied me," I announced. "Now remove my clothes and wash me."

The boyfriend pulled up a patio chair and gestured for me to hold onto the arm of it. He slipped my sandals off and unbuttoned my pants, tenderly peeling them off my legs, then deftly removed my blouse, and then my panties. He broke character for a moment, looking at me with warm, naughty brown eyes, undoing my bra with one hand. He led me to the shower and made sure the temperature felt good before guiding me in. His hands massaged my whole body with suds and glorious water glinting in the sun. He started with the shoulders and then moved down my back to my waist and hips. His hands were soft and strong and sensual. He kneaded my hips like dough and then did the same to my ass, bending down to run his lips over my cheeks.

"May I?" he asked.

"Yes," I allowed.

He sucked and bit on my ass, shoving his head between my legs and holding my thighs. He nearly knocked me off my feet.

"Watch it!" I lashed out.

"So sorry," he said, standing up, pressing his body behind mine, snaking his hands around me until they cupped each breast.

"Perhaps you'd like to take it from behind?" he asked. "Standing up?"

He was toying with me, testing the edges of our game. I was getting super turned on, playing this role of the bitch when all along we both knew he could, at any moment, turn the tables and assume control. I tried to keep it together and maintain my dominance.

"Suck me off first," I ordered.

"Suck *you* off?" he chided. "I didn't know ladies called it that."

"I'll call it whatever I want," I snapped, and choked on a giggle, suddenly caught by how silly the whole thing was.

I suppressed my laughter, trying to cover it by clearing my throat, and pushed his head down quicker than I meant to, so that he didn't see me breaking character.

He got on all fours and looked up at me with a devious smile.

He began by licking my twat in fleshy thrusts. His nails dug into my thighs. I pivoted to get under the water and then pushed his head down. "Lower," I ordered.

He dropped to the floor and grasped my calves, licking my labia lips from underneath. I arched my back so that the water pressure fell right on my clit. It was exhilarating to have that sensation while he was licking me. The image of a car on jacks came to mind, and I thought about how he was licking my undercarriage. I started to laugh but stifled it. *Not in character*, I silently corrected myself.

With a subtle amount of squatting, I could get the water to hit me deliriously in the clit while the boyfriend's mouth worked my pussy hole and lips over. Not a bad way to start a date! I started to moan, but then stopped myself. Better to seem rigid to play the part.

I don't usually come standing up, but the wave of my first orgasm started to build and then gained speed rapidly. It tumbled inside of me and I squatted tiny little thrusts into his face over and over as I came.

"Mmm," he said, licking his lips once I was done. He stood up, shook out his legs, grabbed me from behind, turned me around, and pressed me to the shower wall.

"Can I offer you a finger?" he asked, trailing his index down my butt crack.

"I'll take one, two, then three, followed by a cock," I said.

He nudged my legs apart and slipped a finger inside me.

I gripped the shower door and hung on. Two fingers, then three, and I was really into it. My legs were starting to feel like mush. I wanted that cock so bad.

"Stroke it with your other hand," I commanded.

"Stroke what?" he asked.

"Your fucking cock, you idiot," I snarled.

"Oh," he said. He grabbed ahold of his member while keeping the rhythm of fucking me. I could feel the bump of his hand hit me in the ass with each stroke, and I loved it.

"Fuck me," I ordered. "Now!" I was still holding onto the top of the door. The water was running down my back like a waterfall.

He yanked my hips back, placed his foot along the inseam of mine, and entered my cunt from behind. His cock was the perfect amount of big for me. It stretched me to the max. I wanted him to fuck me hard and never stop.

We were both bucking frantically from the get go. He held onto my ass like a water skier on the line, pounding away. "Give it to me!" I yelled. "I like it rough."

He delivered. He grunted and hurled his body into mine like waves whipping in a hurricane. I furiously jiggled my ass, wanting it to go on and on.

My legs were quaking. I was getting dizzy with lust and deliverance. My fingers were stiff from gripping the door. My pussy was on fire from the pounding and the stretch and the friction. And still I wanted more. "Don't stop!" I grunted through gritted teeth.

He held my ass like a precious vase, and then crushed it with his cock.

Again and again and again.

I could feel his whole body start to twitch and jerk as he pulled out fast and came in great heaping spurts all over the shower. I felt the warm splat against my ass and the slippery drip down my leg. He pulled me close and rubbed his body against mine, and we stepped fully into the shower stream to wash off. More soap and suds. He massaged my shoulders, my arms, my legs.

I felt like breaking character and just being myself. Getting the shit fucked out of you is a sure thing to change your attitude.

"Let's go swimming!" I said brightly, and I grabbed his hand.

The game was over.

Now we could play.

We ran naked onto the dock and threatened to push each other in but neither did. He just gave me an impish grin and leapt off the dock, splashing into the water. The sun was bright pink and the sky was all fuchsia, the water dark blue. I plunged in behind him and we tread water and splashed at each other, giggling.

I swam around in the water a bit, stretching my legs and arms, feeling the cool water caress my tenderized pussy, thrilling in the freedom of my strokes and the fresh, dark liquid around me. I floated on my back and admired the spectacular sky.

In the twilight, the boyfriend was lounging on a rock in the low water. I swam toward him and motioned for him to join me out a little deeper. We came to where the water hit our chests and embraced. He lifted me up and I wrapped my legs around him, feeling his upturned cock against my belly. My hips rolled, grinding my clit against his prick. He held me there, his cock pinned between us, the water making me light enough to carry. I kept rocking my hips while he held my ass, and when I couldn't wait anymore, I reached down and stuffed his cock into me. My pussy sucked him in. He sucked on my nipples, one at a time, while I rode him in the water.

While we fucked, the sky changed from electric pink to lavender to dim silver. The trees around the water grew black, a ragged edge against the dusky sky. I was too spent to come again and I didn't care. It just felt so good to be filled up and grinding against him. And it felt so good to be held in the water, to be carried like that.

When we climbed out of the water, we had no towels, so we just shook like dogs and scampered around, comically forcing the water off our bodies. We grappled with getting our clothes on with wet skin and scrambled back to his truck. "Wait," he said, holding out his hand to bring me around to the bed of the truck. He threw down a blanket and we lay there in the bed of the truck, watching the sky darken to azure and then indigo, waiting for the first evening star to glint into our vision.

"There it is," I called out, tracing it with my finger.

We scanned the sky for planets and constellations, resting our backs after all that exertion. It felt like everything and nothing at once, to live in a body. I could feel my skin tingling, my blood coursing with an effervescent vitality, and I could barely feel the edges of me, hardly feel the line of my own skin separating me from the black night, as if I were floating, as if I were hardly here at all.

"Want to go get that drink now?" he asked me.

I imagined a bar, bumping with music and bodies.

"Nah, I don't think so," I replied.

"Maybe another time?"

"Sure," I said. "Another night." I sighed and felt profoundly at peace in the world for a brief beat. "This one ends here."

Abecedarian Orgy

A is moaning loudly while being fucked from behind by B, who is being pounded in the ass by C while D fondles C's rhythmically swinging balls. D is on his knees with his cock in E's mouth. While E is sucking off D, she is getting licked upside the na-na by F. G is watching from the corner, fondling herself, while H and I scissor on the wood floor with a shared two-sided dildo, where a big puddle is growing. H has her mouth on A's cunt, and she keeps her lips clasped over A's hoochi lips while the thrusting continues from B. "Gimme your cock," G says hungrily to J, who is standing in front of her with a gleam in his eye and a gleam at the tip of his dick. "Do you want me to fuck you?" he asks. "No, I want your dick in my mouth," she insists. He walks over and delivers his short bobbing cock to her wet mouth. He starts to move his hand to her clit, and she pushes it away. "Okay," he says, "you just keep touching yourself. I like that. Oh, that feels good." I screams aloud, "I need an ass to grab!" and K scoots over from where she is rimming L a foot away. She holds L's chest and brings them both over to I, wiggling her fanny for I to grab. "Oh, fuck!" I exclaims as she comes again, slicking the floor. M is straddling N's thick silicone cock on a chair, slowly grinding on it up and down like some kind of beautiful, levitating, churning sex machine, and N has their head tipped back with a drooly expression and their hands all over M's bountiful tits. Behind N, O rubs N's tiny nipples in swirly circles and covers their neck and ears in licks and kisses. Behind O, P is hunched down, licking O's legs ankle to thigh and getting close to the juicy spot, but waiting. P has a butt plug in her ass that is getting manipulated by Q, who is gearing up to fuck her in that exact hole once she's worked up enough. Q is blindfolded with nipple clamps on and a gag in his mouth. He starts to rub P's clit to amp up the heat. Watching all this is R, who is having his balls handled and his cock pumped by S, while T pummels S from behind. U is holding onto R's hips and fucking him in the ass while T fucks S, and suddenly R is coming, and then S is coming, and then T and U, and then everyone is gasping and squirting and shrieking and moaning, and V is recording it all on audio, and W is massaging V's breasts while trying to suck all the cum out of V's vag, and X is grinding against W, who has Y's cock pinned between their thighs, and Z, who is too shy to do anything but stay close-ish to X and W's warm writhing bodies, to feel their heat and listen to all the groaning and thrusting and pumping and arching and spilling and spraying, Z begins to just dance a little bit, a swaying of hips, a light step on the floor, feeling like the one steady spot in the fray—all of it connected, like an organism unfurling.

In the Scrum

YOU KNOW HOW they say if you're nervous to imagine everyone naked? It's a great idea, really takes the edge off. I just don't recommend it before a rugby scrimmage.

Turns out it's very hard to keep your eye on the ball when all you can see through your x-ray vision is naked rugby babes. The field becomes a constellation of dancing taints, dripping pussies like squashed flowers, dazzling assholes, and dangling arbors of bush. Oh, those ample asses, the splayed hindquarters of eight luscious thick-thighed, muscly women. I can't keep my eyes off their spread haunches, their jiggling buttocks as they shift their weight foot to foot in anticipation of the play.

I'm anticipating some play. You'd better believe it. I've got my eye on that dirty little scrum-half. My hands are empty waiting to catch you, sweetheart. Come be mine. My heart is racing. My pussy is creaming my shorts. I'm eyeing every one of your moves. Those swift, deft motions you make to dodge those other girls. How you hustle my way.

Lemme see you sweat. Your eyes on that ball, your hips shoving those hot, steamy, sweatyhind quarters left and right. You push the others aside as you run to me, your eyes clear, your mouth one tight line with your tongue poking out. Oh, I'll put that tongue to use. You naughty, saucy, little rugger, watch out, you're in my line of fire, I'm cumming right for you.

Leigh's Fiftieth

AFTER SHANNON AND Leigh's big dick day to celebrate Shannon's fiftieth, once things went back to normal—the cake eaten, the crumbs swept clean, the kids put to sleep—and the two of them were alone in bed together, they mused over their favorite moments, and all the sensations, and what a sweet guy Derek was, what a total score. Shannon praised Leigh for her good instincts and how she made the whole thing a surprise.

"I love that you gave me sausage for my birthday, you sweetie," Shannon mumbled, kissing Leigh on the nose, "You are so thoughtful."

"Did I get the right kind of guy?" Leigh asked, looking for a little more validation and applause, "because I remembered that you liked Benicio and I was trying to find a guy with a bit of a similar style."

"He was perfect," Shannon confirmed. "You are perfect. You even brought dildos just in case. I feel so nurtured . . ." Shannon purred as she fell asleep.

Leigh lay in bed trying to make sense of it all. She hadn't been sure of any of it, whether it would happen, how she'd feel watching her wife get fucked, and by a dude no less, how she'd feel participating in it. In fact, she'd hardly thought about that part at all until it was upon her, she'd been so focused on Shannon. Now that it had happened and was floating around in her memory bank and still seeping through her body, she took a minute to check in with herself. *Had I wanted that too?* she asked herself honestly. *Yes, I had. I had wanted to please Shannon and delight her. I guess I, too, had wanted some new delights and sensations, I just hadn't admitted it to myself, or to Shannon. Am I hiding something from myself?* she inquired.

Be brave, she instructed her deeper self. *Come on, be honest. What would I want if I could have anything in the world?* An image came into her mind. Her mouth was on Shannon's pussy and she was getting fucked simultaneously in the cunt and the ass by two guys. *Whoa,* Leigh thought. *I didn't know I had it in me. No pun intended,* she chuckled.

***

The next day, Leigh pitched it to Shannon.

"I know what I want for my birthday," Leigh announced in the morning, as they each stood before their sink and mirror doing their daily routines.

"Oh, yeah, honey, what's that?" Shannon asked absently.

"I want double penetration while I go down on you."

"Oh."

"With Derek and one of his friends."

"Ohh. Okay, babe," Shannon said with what sounded like surprise, and perhaps a bit of reluctance.

"Is that okay with you?" Leigh asked.

"Yeah," Shannon confirmed, "I just kinda thought that I was the dirty girl, and you were more, I don't know . . . responsible?"

"Babe," Leigh said sternly, "No. We are gonna have to bust that myth."

"Okay."

"Your birthday bang unleashed my wild side. Okay?"

"Okay." Shannon still sounded a little nervous.

"So, let's roll with it!" Leigh said cheerily. "I think it's good for us."

***

Shannon reached out to Derek.

"So, we were wondering if you'd like to do something like that again . . ." she rambled into the phone. "See, it's Leigh's birthday next month, and she's thinking, well, not that this has to always be a birthday thing, I mean, how silly, we're not children, oh god, of course we're not children, I just mean, it's a reason to do it, but not the *only* reason to do it . . . do it," she repeated. Shannon paused to catch her breath, allowing Derek the opportunity to rescue her, which he did gladly.

"It was really fun, Shannon. I'd be down to do it again. You thinking the same kinda thing?"

"Uh, well," Shannon went on, relieved, but still nervous. "Um, would you have any interest in bringing a friend?" she asked, adding quickly, "Another guy!"

"Huh." Derek paused. "Lemme think on it. I can . . . get back to you?"

"Yes!" Shannon announced. "We were thinking maybe next month? Or over the holiday? Leigh's birthday is the twenty-first, so maybe some time close to that."

"Okay, cool, I'll see what I can work out," Derek said. "Should I call you back on this number?"

"Yes, please," Shannon said, taking a deep breath. "It's a surprise. Well, sort of. But, yes."

***

Shannon remained nervous. Adding one guy was her fantasy, but adding two? She hadn't even considered that. What Leigh was asking for was some porn star shit. On the one hand, she was impressed. But also, intimidated. What was this new wild side of Leigh's? She hadn't really unleashed the beast before. Shannon should like it. Why was she a little freaked out?

Meanwhile, Leigh seemed to go about her life merrily, every once in a while giving Shannon a secret smile, sultry and lascivious, sometimes flashing her a gaping mouth with eyeballs rolled back in their sockets like a brief glimpse into an epic orgasm, and once, when the kids weren't looking, poking her tongue into her cheek and placing her hand in front of her mouth, miming a blow job, followed by a wicked cackle.

Shannon stewed on this change in Leigh and wondered if it was menopause. Didn't some women get extra horny in their fifties? Or was it more common to lose one's sex drive entirely? Shannon couldn't remember. Both sounded bad at the moment. How would she ever keep up with the new Leigh?

Derek called back a week later and said he had a friend, an honorable guy who was really respectful, got tested regularly, and was into a foursome. They set a date. Same hotel, the afternoon before Leigh's big day. *She'd still be forty-nine when they sixty-nined,* Shannon chuckled to herself. Maybe it would all work out okay. What did they have to lose? Leigh seemed really excited. Shannon hadn't told her any details, just that it was on and that she was working it out.

They showed up at the hotel early. This time they got the suite with the kitchenette so there'd be room for four with enough chairs and all. Both took showers and dried their hair, passing the one hair dryer back and forth playfully, surprising the other with locker room style blasts of hot or cold air to the ass, as if they were kids tussling. Shannon started up the playlist she'd prepared, which would kick off with Beyoncé's "Naughty Girl," and move through some of the raunchier Tove Lo songs, the sexiest Rihanna, a little "Feeling Myself," and the incomparable "WAP." That ought to set the mood.

"So . . . who's joining us?" Leigh asked, flipping her hair.

"I honestly don't know," Shannon admitted, "I left it to Derek. He's bringing a friend. I hope that's okay."

"Wait," Leigh said, "you haven't seen a picture or talked to the extra guy or anything?"

"Oh shit, was I supposed to?" Shannon panicked. "Baby, I don't know what I'm doing. This is new to me."

"It's okay, it's okay," Leigh consoled her. "This is our decision. We can just say no if it doesn't feel right. Let's just be open to it and see."

"On the plus side, this time we waxed," Shannon said.

"That's right, baby, I'm ready for this. Gimme that smooth ass grundle. Come here." Leigh brought Shannon into her arms and swayed with her to the music. She tipped her head back to kiss her and ran her hands down over her ass. "I'm so glad you got me this birthday present, my love. Let's have an adventure!"

Leigh smacked Shannon on the ass and wrestled her to the bed.

Just then there was a knock on the door. Shannon answered it.

***

Derek and his friend stood in the doorway looking fresh and clean and handsome, like two guys picking up their double date. Leigh squealed inside, suppressed it, and let out a stifled cough. Shannon gave her a side-look, and Leigh shared a bright smile with eager eyes. Shannon read her "okay" and welcomed them in.

"This is Jason," Derek introduced his friend. "This is Leigh. And this is Shannon. It's almost Leigh's birthday, right?"

"That's right," Leigh interjected, feeling like a schoolgirl confirming her specialness. She altered her vibe to sound more like an adult, and invited them to sit, offering champagne or a cocktail from the picnic basket Shannon had packed. This time, they'd brought cups too.

Over drinks they got to know each other a little. Quickly the conversation went to sex and preferences. Jason was single, he explained, interested in finding a long-time person someday, probably a cis-woman, but open to anyone. "I think I'm straight, but I don't really know. I wanna expose myself to all types of sexuality and genders and situations, so I can find out what feels natural and instinctive to me."

Shannon explained that she and Leigh fell in love in college as counselors at Girl Scout camp, and after they broke up they were apart for many years before getting back together and then getting married and having kids. Leigh added that they had both dated across the gender spectrum, but mostly identified as lesbians. Shannon chimed in that she ran up against judgement from some community members using the term "lesbian" when technically they were "bisexual," but that she believes identity lies within one's own subjectivity, and everyone gets to choose their queer ipseity.

Derek added that beginning when he was a boy, he was always drawn to lesbians, couldn't tell if he kind of wanted to be one or fuck one, or both, but mostly just had always loved the company of queer women, as friends, family, and also lovers.

Leigh was engrossed in the conversation, feeling really comfortable and drawn in, until she suddenly felt a churning in her pelvis and realized her pussy was going to stage a mutiny if she didn't get laid soon.

She gave Shannon an urgent look. Shannon replied with a patient smile and held out her hand to Leigh. They stood up together and kissed, putting a little extra performative flair into the accompanying groping. Derek and Jason sat there watching.

When Leigh began to kiss her neck, Shannon turned her head to Derek and Jason and began to speak.

"So, when Derek came over last time, we had a threesome, and fooled around and fucked each other just about every which way we could think of, right?"

Leigh giggled and nodded, and Derek nodded his head with a dopey smile. "Yeah."

"But Leigh wants to try a few things she's never done before, right, baby?"

Leigh nodded while kissing Shannon's collarbone and massaging her tits through her shirt.

"She wants double penetration while licking my pussy."

Leigh waited for a reaction. There were no objections, only consent across the board. Shannon continued, "And I have a fantasy in mind I'd like to try too. I call it The Rorschach. Basically, you sit in chairs back-to-back, and we each ride you, so we get to share the experience of bring fucked at the same time face-to-face . . . know what I mean?' Shannon paused and let it sink in. "So, how do those ideas sound to you two?"

Derek and Jason cleared their throats and agreed they each liked these ideas. They looked at each other and seemed to hold back a sort of knuckle bump.

"Leigh," Shannon asked, "anything to add, honey?"

Leigh shook her head, feeling suddenly shy on the outside, but also sensing the wildness inside her expanding rapidly like the Incredible Hulk before he busts through his outfit.

Shannon tossed a big box of condoms onto the nightstand along with a bottle of organic lube, a few butt plugs, an assortment of cock rings, and two vibrators. "Let's be liberal with these, huh?" she pitched to the group, and she cranked up her playlist.

***

Leigh was soon in between Derek and Jason. The making out had begun. Shannon suddenly wished she had brought a cock and harness. It would be so hot to peg one of the guys. Or both. Damnit. Why hadn't she thought this through? Oh well, maybe next time. *Yeah, maybe there will be a next time,* she thought. *Maybe they could make this a regular thing. How would that work?* Shannon was spacing out and missing the orgy. She felt a hard cock press against her ass and snapped back to the present moment.

"Take my clothes off," she ordered the group. They swarmed her and did just that.

First, Leigh asked for Derek to fuck her on her back. She wanted Shannon and Jason to watch. That lasted only a few hot minutes before Leigh commanded that Shannon come kneel over her face so she could suck her pussy. When Jason saw that, he wanted to jump in, so he kneeled in front of Shannon and began to massage her tits. Shannon immediately took him into her mouth, so that now she was sucking Jason's cock while Leigh was sucking her pussy while getting pounded by Derek. Easy first arrangement!

Wanting to keep switching it up, Shannon and Jason toppled

onto the bed next to them, Jason lying next to Leigh. Shannon climbed on top. She loved riding cock and Leigh knew it. That was most often how she liked it when Leigh wore a cock at home. But this was the first time Shannon was riding someone else's cock while watching her wife take one too.

Leigh was sweating and swearing as Derek's gorgeous cock wove in and out of her. Shannon pounded Jason as hard she could. The whole scene was so arousing, Shannon felt a paroxysm of lightning zap her g-spot, and she came with a huge gasp all over Jason. Fluids spilled over his tight abs. He was wowed. "Fucking hot," he exclaimed. And then he pumped into her while her pussy clenched and tightened, sucking him in. Shannon came again, with a howl.

"Don't come, don't come," Leigh begged both Jason and Derek. "Keep it hard, make it last. Here, use a cock ring?"

Derek declined. But Jason decided to put one on.

Leigh asked for what she wanted. "What's the best position so you can both fuck me at the same time?"

Jason and Derek both stripped their condoms off and put new ones on. Jason hopped back on the bed and lay on his back, the cock ring clenching his long, pretty shaft right at the base. He motioned for Leigh to get on top of him. Leigh climbed up but didn't mount him yet. Derek took a fistful of lube and was running his hand slickly up and down his thick, rubbered dick. He reached for one of the butt plugs, lubed it quickly, and inserted it into Leigh's asshole. She groaned.

"Fuck I love that." She lowered herself onto Jason's cock. "Oh!" she gasped as the tip reached deep inside her. "Fuck me," she said, in seeming disbelief. She'd yell it like a proclamation later.

Her pussy was full of cock, her ass splayed, her tits pendulous. "Shannon!" she grunted, "come here." Shannon dutifully climbed up and straddled Jason. Leigh gave her pussy a lick from the front, but the position didn't quite work. They awkwardly tried to figure out a way for Leigh to access Shannon's pussy from a good angle. "Baby, maybe you just focus on these two for a sec, and then we'll see, okay?"

"Okay," Leigh concurred between heavy breaths.

Jason was softly pumping his hips into her while Derek was sliding the butt plug in and out. Shannon grabbed a vibrator and lay down where she had a good view. The buzzing began, and Shannon started to grunt and moan.

Derek asked Leigh if she was ready, and she said yes. He removed the plug and licked her asshole a little bit, and then he began to stuff the tip of his cock inside. Leigh yelled for him to wait. "Don't take it out, just lemme catch my breath." Derek stilled with his cock inserted about an inch into Leigh's ass. Jason slowed his pumping down. Leigh had a sweaty game face on. She breathed a few heaving moments, and then said, "Yes. Okay. Now!" And Derek went in.

And Jason went deep. And Leigh was getting it from both of them at once. Just as she'd asked. "I love it, I love it, I love it," she crooned, gasping and writhing and moaning.

Shannon came quick and hard with the vibrator and this scene before her. She scurried over and slid her hand between Jason's crotch and Leigh's to rub Leigh's clit while she was getting doubly fucked. "OH, FUCK!" Leigh exclaimed.

Leigh came so hard she went silent and her eyes rolled back in her head. Her tits were convulsing and her mouth was open in a long fugue of ecstasy that looked kind of like agony. Shannon's mouth fell open. She'd never seen Leigh do this before.

When Leigh finally snapped out of it, she pleaded, between breaths, "More, more, more." They were still inside her. Derek held her ass tight while he started back up again, not pumping this time, but using a spiraling dip motion, a slow twist. "Go," he said to Jason, and Jason began to plunge again, playing with his angle and speed, revving up the tempo with Leigh's sounds, arching deeper when she begged for it.

Leigh came again, this time squeaking and squealing. You could see it rolling through her like a sound wave. Toward the end of it, Derek bucked harder into Leigh's rump, coming with a long snarl of expletives, and then Jason came with a huge "Ahhhh," and everyone was heaving and sweaty and trying to tame their wild heartbeats.

The foursome rolled apart for some air. Leigh lay on her back staring up at the ceiling, starry-eyed. "Baby, come now," she whimpered. Shannon came over and began to stroke her torso, her ribs, her tits. "You okay, love?"

"Sit on my face," Leigh instructed in a woozy voice.

Shannon did as she was told.

Leigh clenched Shannon's hips and sucked her pussy with more gusto than usual. Derek leaned down and sucked Leigh off at the same time. Leigh was fucking every part of Shannon's pussy with her mouth all at once, each labia, the clit, the whole vulva. Shannon couldn't figure out how or what Leigh was doing with her mouth, but it felt incredible and she could feel the orgasm building deep within. It would come to the brim and then recede like a tide just before spilling. It did that a few times, while Shannon made animalistic noises and Leigh gripped her ass tighter, cramming all of Shannon into her mouth, using her chin and nose to add to the pressure. Shannon tipped over the edge, coming like an upturned bucket, dousing Leigh's mouth and face with pussy water.

Leigh spluttered to a halt and wiped her face with the back of her hand, her eyes gleaming like a madman. Then she came hard, with a wail and convulsions. The beast had certainly been unleashed. "Holy shit, baby," Shannon exclaimed in disbelief.

"A little more," Leigh demanded, pushing Derek away and wrestling Shannon onto her back. Leigh straddled her and stuck her ass up in the air like it was during the double penetration. She went down on Shannon from this angle, like a wolf. Shannon was gyrating and yowling. "One of you bring your cock!" Leigh instructed, only removing her mouth from Shannon's throbbing cunt to give the order.

Jason came over with a slick cock and entered Leigh's puckered little butthole. She gasped. And then she rode him harder, twerking into his hips while she ate Shannon out.

After that everyone needed some water, another drink, and to take turns standing in front of the fan. They shared giggles and accolades and astonishment. Leigh hopped in the shower. Shannon followed. And then all four of them were stumbling around in the glass box, kissing and rubbing and dripping together. Leigh reached her hand into Shannon's pussy and began to fuck her right where she liked it. Shannon gushed all over her hand, splatting in the shower and crying with pleasure again and again, her knees buckling. Jason held her up. Derek kissed her neck. And Leigh kept fucking her. Shannon just kept coming.

"Okay, I want my Rorschach," Shannon insisted, once everyone was towel dried and ready for more. While the guys took two dining chairs and placed them back-to-back, Shannon consulted quietly with Leigh on preference. Leigh opted for Jason, and let Shannon take Derek, since they hadn't fucked yet this time.

The men were waiting to be told what to do, and once they were ordered to sit, they did. "Should I tie your ankles to the chair?" Shannon asked. Jason said, "Yes, please" and Derek shook his head. Shannon stripped Leigh's belt from her jeans on the floor and tied Jason's ankles tight to the chair legs. He let out a pleased sigh. Both women rolled condoms over cocks and slid some lube up and down the shafts.

And then they each climbed on.

There was a chorus of moaning as each woman found her rhythm and each guy got his cock squeezed and stroked by a hot pulsing pussy. The clamor of pleasure was amplified by the smacking of taints on balls.

Leigh hitched her hips forward to make her cunt tug on Jason's cock in an extra arousing way. She gripped his shoulders and met Shannon's eyes.

Shannon was riding Derek with short little grunts, and she reached for Leigh, gripping Leigh's hands on Jason's shoulders. She startled when Derek took her nipple into his mouth, and let out a yelp of revelry. She could feel her clit getting stimulated by the hard thump of Derek's pubic bone as she hammered him. Her pussy lips were doing that thing where they were so wet and puffed up, they were slipping as she fucked him. It felt immeasurably pleasurable.

***

Leigh loved getting to watch her wife fuck a guy while she herself was fucking a guy. This position was genius. She pressed the rungs of the chair with the arches of her feet and got more traction and weight that way so she could pound Jason even harder. He tipped his head back and his mouth dropped open. He could hardly deal, she could tell. He smiled at her with a satisfied grin and egged her on with his eyes. Both men, who had exerted so much effort in all the other positions, were fully passive now, reduced to their submissive cocks. Leigh tightened her pussy muscles around Jason's cock, thwacked her ass against him with a rapid rhythm, and felt his cock illuminate her from taint to crown. Goddamn if she didn't feel like she was made of electricity.

A few more orgasms for all, and the afternoon was winding to a close. The four of them rested in the king bed, entwined and sweaty, already reminiscing about their favorite moments. They applauded Leigh's assertiveness and assured her how hot it was that she asked for what she wanted. Jokes were shared over the Rorschach, and claims made that it would go down in history under that name thanks to Shannon. Together they celebrated the openness and courtesy they had all brought to the date, and marveled at each other's prowess, flexibility, and range.

After a shower and a snack from the charcuterie plate that Shannon brought, they hugged and kissed and said goodbye. Everyone was in agreement to meet again.

"Hey, Jason," Derek joked, "when do you turn 33?"

Inventing a Form

Can we feel this out, be together today, tonight, and then just see
what comes of it?
With no expectations or presumptions or requirements?
Can we just share intimacy, love, heal some old wounds—
Mouth to mouth, a honeylike salve?

And when I first kissed her it was on her thumb. I lifted her hands and praised them. These hands were the hands that had just helped me move all my belongings from one apartment to the next. Our eyes met, and I didn't break our gaze to kiss first her thumb, then the side of her palm, her wrist, her inner arm where the skin is soft as silk, and then the other hand, wrist, arm. She leaned in to kiss my lips. I beamed at her and gently pressed my thumb to her chin. "I want to," I said. "But not yet."

I nuzzled her neck and pulled her close to me. I wanted to know something of her before we kissed mouth to mouth. For some reason I don't know or understand, I often dissociate when I start to make out with someone. And with her I wanted to be fully present. I needed to ground us through our bodies first. She moaned while I kissed her neck, and I paused and took a step back so our eyes could meet. Hers were sparkling. Mine felt like they were lit with small fires. I ran my hands over her neck, tracing the muscles, fingers light like feathers.

I traced her hairline and the bridge of her nose, the divot over her lips, her collarbone. *I am in a thing with this woman*, I thought. *We are sharing something. This is what I've always wanted.* But I had to remove any expectation I was tempted to put on it. I had to cleave this moment from any fantasy that might take me out of it.

She wrapped her arms around my ribcage in a hug. We just felt each other like that for a long while, heart to heart. My hand stroked her hair. Her fingers ran down the back of my neck over and over. My breath was going through waves of soft and ragged. Under my dress, my pussy was a swollen plum.

"Will you remind me this is just today?" I asked.

"This is just today," she said. "I don't need or want or expect anything from you. We are just doing this now, okay? No other plans. Let's just feel it out and see."

I breathed a huge sigh of relief. "You keep talking like that, I'm gonna come."

She laughed. "Oh, I have other ways of making you come."

***

Later, we were in bed spent and sweaty, nestled body to body.

I'm scared of dying from wheels going too fast.
What I mean to say is, I'm scared of losing control.

I'm scared of falling off the edge of a cliff.
What I mean to say is, I'm scared of losing what I love.

She joked about taking her boat across the river to see me again some time and taking it through the delta out to sea together. "Bring some extra rope," I said.

Bring your salt, I thought.
Bring your brine.
Bring your heaving rhythm, your gasp, the glint of light off the water in your eyes.
Bring your teeth like coral.

When she had me tied to the bed, and the mattress was a soggy puddle and my cheeks were red, my eyes wild, my pussy fucked to perfection, she asked if she could kiss me now.

I had no hands to hold her, no legs to wrap around her, no more than a few inches to move my neck. So instead I just lay there. Surrendered. "Yes. Please kiss me." It worked better for me that way. She broke the spell.

I had undressed her slowly. Run my fingers down her spine. Lifted her arms to inhale her scent. Brushed my lips against her nape. I knew a little something of her history, sensed the crust that had formed around her tenderness from being hurt.

What I wanted was to give her healing. What I wanted was for this to be different in every way. Eyes held. Hands cherished. Pussy licked by passion, not by greed.

"I've never been held like this," she whispered.
The tears came then.
And then my hands.

"I've never been seen like this," I told her.
Came her mouth. And her arms. And her hips.

She left the way she came in, through the doorway, in a slant of sunlight, a bracket of blue river shining. She walked over the hill and down to her truck. I tasted her like the last bite of summer strawberry pie. When you want it to linger in your mouth forever.

I Am a Woman Fueled by Eros

I AM A woman fueled by eros. Don't mistake my passion for need or greed. I am hungry for sensuality and pleasure. I feed on it. It juices me up, even while I sleep.

I awake to the soft sheets and her breath on the back of my neck. I awake to her arms around me and my ass pressed to her hips. I awake to sunlight streaming through the windows and the birds bustling outside, a light breeze in the air, carrying the scent of last night's love-spiced bodies. I awake to a teeny tiny hard-on tugging on my clit.

I wiggle to face my lover, who is sleeping soundly, her lips parted, the gap in her teeth just visible, the little bow of her mouth open like a squashed teardrop. The down on her cheek glints in the light. She sighs, the rhythm of her sleep rolling through her ribcage.

Her ear is like a little shell washed up on the beach. Her eyes are spiked with long black lashes. Her cheek is a little flushed from the furnace of my body heating up her core. Her breasts are soft between her elbows, her arms slack, released from their hold of me.

I like my lover to awaken to sex. Her sex. My mouth on it. I sidle down her body with the subtlest, softest maneuvers to keep her consciousness dormant, brushing my lips to make her moan but not rouse while I get to my buried treasure.

Morning cunt is an extra special treat. She's been steeping in her nectar, the marinade of last night's lovemaking. Her pussy is sealed with all that lovely sap tucked inside. I lay soft little kisses and extra light licks of my tongue down the length of her belly, hearing her moan in her sleep, knowing that her body is gathering ooze inside.

"You are the one I pick, for now," I whisper into her cunt, "to share my passion and sensuality." I murmur poetry to her body parts, one at a time.

"Yours is the cunt I dream of and crave first thing in the morning."

I kiss the center seam of her.

"I fall asleep with your salt on my lips," I mumble as I run light lips over her navel.

"I must have you again now," I whisper to her thighs.

"I belong inside you," I breathe into her bush.

"I can't get enough of you," I hiss into her hipbone.

I make my tongue very soft.

I grunt with admiration, wet my lips, and place my silky tongue at the little rosebud of her clit. I let it linger there, still, my breath warm against her cunt, my tongue beating its own vitality against her pleasure button. She sighs and shifts her hips. I challenge myself to leave it there still as long as I can. As long as I can resist taking her. Then, I lick up the seam of her cunt like I'm scooping the white from an Oreo. Still in dreamland, she whimpers.

We always fall asleep in each other's arms, spent from a night of lust and ardor. I love to fall asleep with our bodies entangled. I love to breathe her in while I sleep all night. I love to feel her neck fuzz tickle my nose when I'm the big spoon, and then when we shift (because we are switchy, even like that), I love to feel her lips graze my hair, the tips of my ears, my shoulders. I want to be held by her and in her and around her and together with her. I want to have to take a minute to figure out whose limbs are whose.

I make my hands extra gentle when they hold her hips. I press my nose, my lips, my tongue into her pussy. "Baby," she mumbles through her dreams, longing in her voice, delight germinating behind the veil of slumber.

I lick her pussy lips with long, soft tongue strokes. This, because it is morning. This because she still sleeps, and I want to coax her from her dream state to a climax without ever waking. When she starts to mewl like a kitten, I let her ride that out a little longer and then I change my technique. I rub my tongue back and forth over the hood of her clit, feeling for the root to swell and get harder. I lick small strokes up the sides of her clit and run my tongue down the crevices between her labia. She exhales and twists in her sleep, crooning my name.

I loll my tongue in circles around the hood, making little spirals, wider and harder at the base and softer and lighter and smaller at the tip of her clit. I find myself grinding against the bed, mashing my pussy into the sheets, wishing I had a thick silicone cock to enter me while I massage my lover's morning clit with my mouth.

It's good enough to imagine it. I can almost feel the hard tip entering me. The thought of it sends a thrill up my spine. I imagine hands pulling my hips back, a steady grip, a persistent thrust. *Mmm,* I sigh into her cunt. I mean it about the imaginary cock, and I mean it about the taste of her, warm and fragrant, seasoned like the best kind of armpit, that peppery spiced aroma that cranks my heat up to ten.

I won't stop until you come, I think-whisper into her beautiful burrow.

I lick a little harder, faster, more persistently. She writhes against my hands, which are now holding her down, tosses her head back and forth. "Ohhh," she murmurs. I continue. I stroke her clit with my tongue until I can feel it about to burst. Then I run small wild circles around it and tug on it with suction, just a bit. She jerks and sucks her teeth.

"Come on, baby," I insist as I slip a finger inside. She oohs and aahs and rocks against my hand. More fingers. More rocking. More pressure. More speed. More, more, more.

"I want more of you," I mumble into her magic little vortex.

It's easy to get her to come like this, with my fingers inside her, my tongue on her clit—the thing is, I want us to come at the same time, so I have to get myself there too. Her taste, the delicious love tonic of her cum boiling inside, the aromatic fragrance of her lust as it seeps off her thighs and into my nostrils, the way my hair falls over her gorgeous belly, the breeze tickling my skin, the image in my mind of the cock entering my hole as I fuck her, the sensation of being taken as I take her, I can feel it in my body, a semblance of it happening, and it cranks me up. All of it lifts me higher and higher, closer to my climax.

She reaches down then to grab my hair and pull my head into her pussy, mashing my face in, creaming me with her juices.

"Anything, anything . . ." she purrs, "you get anything you want."

I slide my hand within her. I lick her clit and tug on it. She bucks against me. I start to unravel. A hole like quicksand in my cunt, and I'm coming, I'm coming, I'm coming—right along with her. Together we ride the waves.

An Interplay of Oppositions

Every week I stayed after class to ask Andy questions, but mostly I was just watching his lips move. The crest of his upper lip was a heart-shaped cleave of pink under a swath of light stubble. Tiny dimples winked at the corners of his mouth. While he was talking, his eyes danced away in philosophic reverie and then returned to me with a hard glint. *Show me your secrets*, I thought-whispered into his eyes.

When Andy lectured to us about Derrida and the myth of presence I imagined fucking him. *You are inside me*, I said in my head, conjuring his hands around my waist, the hot throb of his cock in my pussy. *Now I'm inside you*, I thought, flipping it, backing Andy up against the wall, grabbing his hips, bending him over.

The last night of class, I stayed after to ask Andy for advice on how to get my paper published. He said it was worth having a long conversation about, and would I like to go have a drink and talk about it further. *Yes.*

We had several drinks, and while our mouths were talking one thing and our minds were talking another, I took off my shoe and rubbed my toes against Andy's shin under the table. I gave him my *I'm so serious* look.

When we left the bar I asked Andy when he was going to invite me back to his apartment. *Right now*, he whispered, and turned and pressed me up against the brick wall and kissed me.

It wasn't a first time kind of kiss. It was a kiss as if we'd been lovers many times before. It was a kiss on a bridge in Paris. It was a kiss in the dark of a throbbing dance party. It was a kiss before, during, after making sweaty desperate love kind of kiss. The bricks scratched against the backs of my shoulders. Andy's knee pressed to the wall, between my thighs. My fingers raked through his hair, up the length of his neck and into the crevices at the corners of his jaw. I traced his cheekbone and inhaled his breath down to my toes.

An hour later Andy was naked and tied to the radiator, and begging for me to stand over him so he could tongue my pussy while the tile floor was stamping little hexagons into his knees. The radiator was on but it wasn't too hot. Still, he had to be careful that he didn't lean against it for too long. I stepped towards him and hitched my skirt up to let the scent of my pussy linger over his face. He stretched to reach me. The intensity of his desire was making me very wet. I could feel a twang of hot lust snaking its way down inside of me. I hovered over Andy's face, swaying my hips ever so delicately. I made us both wait.

I took off the little silk scarf I had tied around my neck and carefully balled it up and stuffed it in Andy's mouth. His eyes got wet when I did that.

I put my face close enough to his neck to feel the steam of his skin and then I breathed a line of heat down the length of him. I made my way down to his belly and then I switched my breath from out to in to take in the scent of him, smoky and spicy and wet. I inhaled a message from each crevice of his belly and groin and balls. His body was talking to me in the loud clamor of the mixed aromas of his sweat. A collage of images flashed through my mind. Andy on the floor on top of me pounding, my mouth open in a gasp. Andy and me up against the kitchen table, my legs splayed, my high heels still on. A close-up of my nipple bulging in the snap of his teeth. A snapshot of cum dripping out of the corner of my mouth. Andy bent over in the shower, my hips pressed to his ass, water pooling in the rifts where our body lines meet. *You're mine*, I whispered. And I ran my lips once lightly along the length of his cock, before I paused for a count of ten, while the images filed themselves like notecards into the storage drawer of my mind.

My lips around Andy's cock, my grip on him slick with spit.

Running my lip lock up and down the shaft of his cock, moaning, I brought him to the edge and then slowed down to enhance the craze and make it last. *Just a little*, I said. *Maybe you'll get more later.*

I took a few steps back from Andy and watched him down there on the floor, with his engorged glistening cock leaping at me from the province of his lap. Now I had his attention. I reached up into my shirt to massage my belly and ribs, scratched my fingernails down the ridge-line of my ribcage and tipped my head back, licked the wet ellipse of my lips. Sliding my shirt to the floor, I left my black lace bra on because it looked so pretty against my smooth skin. Andy was watching the place where my thigh highs gripped my leg girth. My eyes telegraphed the tidal wave of lust building to Andy, his eyes squinting back his desperation.

Undulating my hips and twisting my torso to show Andy all the ways in which I could torque myself to meet him, I slid my panties to the floor and pulled the silk scarf from his warm, wet mouth. *Now you can have me*, I purred. *And maybe I'll untie you later.*

Entre Nous

She was waiting for me in the bathroom. That was the plan all along. She would wait for me in the bathroom, I would excuse myself from the table, and we would fuck like maniacs in the end stall, perfectly silently, me standing on the toilet so that only one set of feet show, then we'd exit one at a time. I'd go back to the table. Mitch would go back to her car and drive home. It seemed like the best solution to having to endure dinner at a stuffy French restaurant with my parents.

Of course she had to gag me. There's no other way I could possibly be quiet. At first, I used to make noises even with the gag, a choking sort of moaning and clucking, but eventually, with some practice, I got accustomed to it, to the thickness it stuffed inside my mouth, its weight against my tongue, reminding me to be silent. Eventually, I could come like a freight train and make not so much as a peep.

It was the noises, I realized, that were taking the intensity out of my pleasure. They were like a slow leak of air from a tiny hole, a way of draining my breath, leaving less energy to go to my pussy where I needed it. I think it was my body's defense mechanism—that my pleasure center was afraid of exploding if it really felt anything and everything it could. But being aware of my power draining is a new thing.

It wasn't until Mitch fucked me in the back stacks of the library one day that it dawned on me to stop being such a loudmouth. Oh, it wasn't just being in the library. I was good at shifting my whimpers and screams to a form of heavy panting in her ear. But even that was funneling my energy outside of my deepest places. It was while she had me pressed up against the stacks of books, my legs straddled, fingers gripping the cool metal ledge of the shelf, getting pounded from behind by Mitch's fist, that my eyes lolled back into focus for one moment, just long enough to land on the spine of a book. *The Power of Silence.* It was an omen dropped like a fishing line into the musty, murky, library basement, and its words jostled in my mind, long after our adventure.

Silence. It gave me something to think about. Not the kind of silence from holding your breath—that can put your power on pause. No. The kind of silence that builds power is what I craved. The kind of silence that comes from breathing not from your mouth, but from deep in your body. That silence. The kind of silent breath that drops like an anvil into your pussy on a deep inhale and shoots like a firework up your spine when you exhale. The kind of silence that allows things of the air to manifest as physical form. Silence that engraves itself into an ecstatic scribbling deep within you. An etching your body traces over and over again, and remembers, as bliss. Silence that makes me rake my fingers down Mitch's back until she bleeds a holy trail of pleasure pain.

So, there we are in the bathroom.

I'm standing on the rim of the toilet. My hands are pressed flat to the cold metal of the stall. My eyes are locked to Mitch's eyes, while her fingers slip in and out of my creamy tingling pussy ever so slowly. She's only giving me a teaser. I know she's packing. *More*, I mouth, silently. She smiles and shakes her head slowly. She starts to rub my clit with her thumb while her fingers keep slowly fucking me. I am getting so hot and I want it more, more, more, so I can explode in sparkling luxury and practice my perfected silent peak. Mitch just smiles at me with her glossy brown eyes. She slows down even more. I give her an exaggerated pouty face and pull my dress down low to show her the spill of my boobs over the lacy edge of my French bra. I know she can't resist that.

She falters, and licks her lips. I start to pinch my nipple and roll it between my fingers. I let my mouth drop open into the shape of silent longing, and arch my back. Mitch shakes her head no, and reaches into her pocket for the gag. Its black leather strap clinches the bulbous ball that will soon be snug in my mouth. She buckles it around my head.

It's a heavy hand holding my tongue. It calms me. It brings me back to my center. Mitch's hand picks up speed. I keep my feet solid against the toilet and continue to press my palms to the walls, while I start to writhe my hips, just ever so slightly towards Mitch's hand. Shifting to meet her like this, in the tiniest most subtle way, always takes me to the next level. While I micro-rock my pelvis back and forth, Mitch's long fingers snake their way deeper into my pussy. I can feel the arch of her finger roaming the canal of my vaj for that soft spongy spot that makes me come like a waterfall. Her thumb is busy rocking against my clit, making it hot and shiny.

Mitch hikes my dress up with one hand and bunches it to the side, grabbing ahold of my hipbone and the dress so she can see me better. She wants to watch my hips fucking her hand and I know it. She wants to smell the ripe, spicy scent of my pussy as it gushes. She wants to see my lace panties stretched taught between the trunks of my thighs. She wants to keep my dress clean because she's thoughtful like that. Mitch widens her fingers inside me and fucks me deeper and I start to lose it. *No sounds, no sounds*, I tell myself. The gag is an anchor in my mouth. A stone that holds me here. An anvil tied to my tongue. I can feel the pleasure, deeper, broader, longer. I can feel my body opening like layers of inaudible bubbles popping, like a thousand roses blooming, every muscle bursting into a quiver. I'm opening, opening, opening. My insides get slick, wide, and start to spill. Cum sloshes out of me like an avalanche. I can feel my pussy convulsing around Mitch's fingers. The shock waves loosen my core to a column of ripples. She doesn't stop.

Mitch keeps fucking me with her hand, deliberate, slow, intentional. I can feel her desire pushing its way into me. She pulls my dress up higher and starts kissing my belly. It feels so good. Mitch. Her tongue teasing the rim of my bellybutton, her breath like a warm chain of kisses along my waist. She licks the edges of my hip bones and nuzzles my bellybutton. And while she kisses me her hand keeps fucking me. I want to tell her to stop, that I have to go back to dinner, that my parents are surely wondering what's taking me so long, that... but I can't do, it, it feels too good. I couldn't anyway, with the gag in my mouth, and the promise of silence between us. I can't say a word.

She knows I need to go back to dinner. The agreement was for the quickest and quietest fuck in bathroom history. Beyond these walls there is a bustling restaurant full of luscious plates of food arriving to tables with tidy elegant place settings, petite vases of flowers, shiny wine glasses, and rich creamy desserts. Mitch notices my attention wavering, at the same time as her internal clock goes off. Mitch is wired liked that. She pulls her hand mostly out of my pussy, just leaves two fingers hooked inside on the edge of my pubic bone. She looks at me with glossy eyes and smiles the most loving, sweetest grin. She gently removes her fingers, giving my pussy a little pat as they leave, as if to say, *see you later*. Her dimples flash as she removes the gag. I stand there, still tingling, as her hands knowingly remake me, guiding my breasts back into their lacy cups, pulling my panties up so tenderly, smoothing my dress down, and combing my hair back into place with her fingers, still fragrant with the aroma of my pussy. She kisses me longingly on the mouth, and slips out the bathroom stall. I imagine her sneaking out the back door of the restaurant, into her truck and driving home. I'll see her later.

I wait a moment, then hop down from the toilet, wash my hands, and notice my face in the mirror, brightly alive and slightly flushed. I leave the bathroom, headed back to the table, with a bigger appetite, ready to compose a night of surprises in store for Mitch.

Acknowledgments

HUGE GRATITUDE TO my readers: Megan Kruse, Holly Goodman, Tracy B, Temim, and Megan Greenauer, for your time and energy, keen eyes, guidance, and support. Thanks to Jan C, B Jones, and Melissa C for your encouragement, Katie P for the inspiration, and Nastashia, Udom, Carter, Kowkie, Kriz, and Leanna for your careful reads, input, and insights. Big thank yous to Jason Grayle for the idea to write a healing story, to both Casey Carpenter and Wayne Bund for the photos, support, and community vibes, and to Alissa Beddow for her fantastic collaboration in graphic design. And thanks to Doug Chase and Kevin Sampsell for the publishing support and opening doors for this book in print.

Cheers of appreciation to my dream editor, Hannah Bennett, and the magnificent crew at Cleis Press. Thank you so much for your dedication, thoughtfulness, and hard work turning this story collection into a book.

Eternal love and homage to those who chiseled a corridor in the labyrinth of erotic writing: the illustrious Kathy Acker, dear Dorothy Allison, Sarah Waters, Jeanette Winterson, Isabella Rossellini, Catherine Millet, Leslie Fienberg, Marguerite Duras, and my darling Lidia Yuknavitch. Admiration and props to these weavers of the lascivious into our arts and culture: Abbi Jacobson and Ilana Glazer, Phoebe Robinson and Jessica Williams, Cardi B and Megan Thee Stallion, Tanya Saracho, Missy Elliott, Joey Soloway, Lizzo, Awkwafina, Lil Nas X, Lucille Bogan, Tribe 8, John Waters, and Amy Sedaris and the team of Strangers with Candy.

To my ancestor Sholem Asch—the original taboo-buster in my family tree, who brought lesbian love to the stage in the early 1900s in Poland, I hope I am honoring your legacy. High fives to you in the ethers, with hugs and gratitude—l'chaim!

Thank you to the lovers who flintstruck my insides, waking me up to myself, and providing the seeds for some of these stories, you know who you are.

So much love and thanks to my Meg, for your eyes on this and your hands on me, my delicious legit switch, sent from the goddesses who wrote our story alongside these and made my dreams come true.

To the rest of you, reading this now: let's keep being curious, open-hearted sensualists. I think we make the world a better place.